The Book of Small Changes

A flash-fiction I Ching

Tim Stevenson

Published by Gumbo Press

First Published 2014 by Gumbo Press
This edition 2016
Printed using CreateSpace.

Gumbo Press
18 Caxton Avenue
Bitterne
Southampton
SO19 5LJ
www.gumbopress.co.uk

Cover design by Tim Stevenson.

A CIP Catalogue record for this book
is available from the British Library

ISBN 978-1495453403

For Michelle, with love.

Contents

Acknowledgements

A big thank you to Calum and Kath Kerr, Vanessa Gebbe, Tania Hershman, Carole Burns, everyone at The Hyde and Alton Writers' Groups and, most of all, Michelle Keefe who critiqued, assisted and informed. Also, my listening, reading and punctuating friends James Walsh, Tom Burnell and Helen Knotts, and to the writers whose work inspired me as I was writing this, Andrew Kaufman, David Sedaris, David Gaffney, Yoko Ogawa and Nik Perring.

Tim Stevenson.
December, 2013.

Introduction

Do you want to know your future?

It's an age-old question born from a fascination with what will happen next, in business, in love, in life, and in death.

Nearly five thousand years ago the Chinese thought they had the answer, the *I Ching*.

The *I Ching* is the oldest of the Chinese classics, dating from around 2,800 BC, and is used to divine the future with the toss of a coin or the counting of yarrow stalks.

In the Edo Period in Japan (1603 - 1868) the *I Ching*, also known as the "Classic of Changes" or "Book of Changes", was widely studied, with over a thousand books published on the subject. These secret teachings were publicized by Rinzai Zen Master, Kokan Shiren and the Shintoist, Yoshida Kanetomo, which is why the cover of this book features the circular Japanese *Ensō*, which symbolizes absolute enlightenment, strength, elegance, the universe, and the void.

The *I Ching* itself is made up of a series of sixty-four symbols or 'hexagrams' that represent each possible outcome from tossing a coin six times. Each hexagram is composed of solid (heads) or broken (tails) lines in two groups of three lines, or 'trigrams' that combine to form the complete hexagram.

These three line trigrams that make up the six line hexagrams are called *Sky, Earth, Thunder, Wind, Water, Fire, Mountain* and *Marsh*. These have special significance within the *I Ching*, as each represents an element of the universe and together they represent the perfection of creation, the totality of all things.

The text of the *I Ching* is a commentary on both the spiritual, moral and universal nature of the hexagram symbols, giving the reader the ability to "delight in Heaven and understand Fate". It seeks to provide symbolic and numerological parallels between the natural world and ourselves, and there have been

11

many interpretations, translations and schools of thought as to what the correct meanings actually are.

This book is another.

The original text for each hexagram is broken down in the following way:

> **The Judgement** – a summary of the meaning of the hexagram as a whole.
>
> **The Image** – a symbolic summary that complements the Judgement.
>
> **The Lines** – a breakdown of the meaning of each line in the hexagram, where a *Nine* refers to a solid line and a *Six* refers to a broken line. Note that the interpretation of the lines starts at the bottom of the hexagram and moves upwards.

To show you what that means, here is an example.

Hexagram 14: Ta Yu - Possession in Great Measure

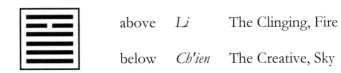

above	*Li*	The Clinging, Fire
below	*Ch'ien*	The Creative, Sky

The Judgement

> Possession in Great Measure.
> Supreme success.

The Image

> Fire in heaven above:
> The image of Possession in Great Measure.
> Thus the superior man curbs evil and furthers good,
> And thereby obeys the benevolent will of heaven.

The Lines

Nine at the beginning means:
No relationship with what is harmful;
There is no blame in this.
If one remains conscious of difficulty,
One remains without blame.

Nine in the second place means:
A big wagon for loading.
One may undertake something.
No blame.

Nine in the third place means:
A prince offers it to the Son of Heaven.
A petty man cannot do this.

Nine in the fourth place means:
He makes a difference
Between himself and his neighbour.
No blame.

Six in the fifth place means:
He whose truth is accessible, yet dignified,
Has good fortune.

Nine at the top means:
He is blessed by heaven.
Good fortune.
Nothing that does not further.

When writing the flash-fictions in this book, I tried to pick a detail from each of the commentaries that would inspire a modern story while keeping the essence of meaning from the original text. This modernisation was sometimes a lot more challenging than it should have been, mostly because the *I*

Ching contains *a lot* of dragons, as you can imagine.

At the end of each story I have included the elements from each commentary that I took for inspiration as I was writing. I hope these snippets of the whole prove enlightening as to where the ideas originated. By the way, the *I Ching* only has sixty-four hexagrams. The last story in this book is not part of this pattern, but an entirely new hexagram of my own creation.

The Game

Take a coin from your pocket.

Have a pen and paper handy then toss the coin.

Draw an unbroken line for "Heads" and a broken line for "Tails". Repeat this six times until you have six lines in a hexagram like the ones opposite.

Find your hexagram in the picture. The number below the hexagram is the story you should read first.

So, do you want to know the future?

(And if you didn't want to play the game, story 65 is for you.)

Tim Stevenson.

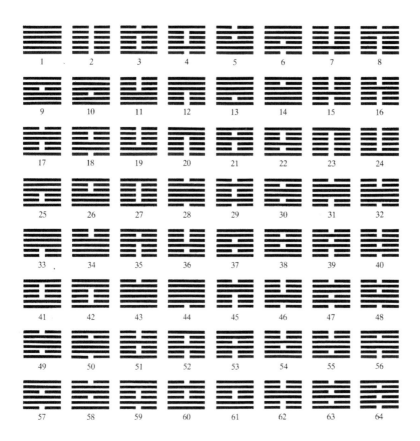

The Book of
Small Changes

The Creative

1. *Ch'ien*

He left his easel and his surfboard in the van and walked down the moonlit beach to find her.

He tried to explain, his words coming from deep within, but still less than she deserved.

"It was unexpected, you know?" he said. "It just happened." He didn't know how to tell her.

He heard the scorn in her sighs.

"I was there, and then she was there and then we were just there together."

She threw water on the sand and soaked his feet.

"We're going to move in, you know, so I'll be working and there'll be no time for…"

She pulled back and flexed her limbs, arched her back, her green dress curling in the breeze, rising up high above his head and filling the sky.

Then she came for him, roaring, screaming, her arms flung open, her white scarves flying from her shoulders in the wind, her body leaping and rolling down towards him on great, wide wings, crashing her desperation on the sand, her salt tears hissing on the beach, her open mouth full of the fire of the setting sun.

He reached down and felt her flinch, ebbing away from his last gentle touch, and knew she'd understood what he'd been trying to say.

The movement of heaven is full of power. Hidden Dragon. At nightfall is mind is beset with cares. There appears a flight of dragons without heads. Good fortune.

The Receptive

2. K'un

The horse led the warrior by the reins, finding the hidden path with careful steps. Surrounding them, the marshland's tall reeds stood motionless, the thin mist parting as the sun, still low in the sky, cast its dull light over this empty place.

Water filled the hollows of their steps and frost clung to the reeds and mud, the heat sucked out of this place by what lay ahead.

Soon the horse and warrior found standing water frozen solid, frogs and nesting birds trapped as they fled.

A desperate snarling carried across the marsh. The mist was alight with distant yellow fire arcing and twisting. The ground shook and the horse stumbled, dropped to its knees, rolled its eyes in terror and refused to go any further.

The warrior placed a blanket over the quivering mare and drew a sword.

Above the reeds vast shapes tumbled, withdrew then crashed together. Claws and breath gouged and burned as the two dragons fought to the end.

Fountains of black and yellow blood sprayed over the earth, but now both animals were tiring, their attacks less frenzied; all the warrior had to do was wait.

Soon a single dragon lay steaming in the mud as the other dragged itself away, its victory writ large in the dark red gouged into its flanks.

The warrior removed her helmet and, with her sword at the ready, crept towards the dying beast.

She filled her bag with the great, yellow teeth, the seeds of her profession, and smiled.

"Dragonslayer indeed," she thought. "Our Kings are fools to think we kill these monsters. These dragons are all males, they sprout and prosper from the ruin of others of their kind and, as with all Kings and powerful men, if you wish one dead, just tempt two close together and be patient."

She watched the surviving dragon take to the sky and disappear, towards the river valleys and the deep forests at the base of the distant mountain. Witch country. Warrior country. Dragon country.

Home.

Her horse approached through the blackened stubble of the reeds and together they watched the dragon's flight until it disappeared.

The Receptive brings about sublime success, furthering through the perseverance of a mare. If the superior man undertakes something and tries to lead, he goes astray; but if he follows, he finds guidance. When there is hoarfrost underfoot, solid ice is not far off. Hidden lines. One is able to remain persevering. Dragons fight in the meadow. Their blood is black and yellow.

Difficulty at the Beginning

3. Chun

Retirement flat. The words made Enid's false teeth itch. An assisted, monitored, managed, senior citizen, ground floor living flat; plus it was as far away from her children as they could possibly manage.

She'd been thinking up some extra-special guilt to pour into their answering machines but that could wait. Right now she had bigger plans.

She peered through the net curtains and waited until her neighbours came back from the school run.

The cars parked and opened their doors and there, on the pavement with her walker, was Enid.

She missed the edge of the kerb and fell, her extra thick padded jacket taking most of the damage as she carefully folded one leg beneath her, lowered herself slowly, but not unconvincingly, down onto the roadside and pulled her walking frame on top of her.

"Oooooh!" Across the road a woman gasped. It was music, a simple introduction to the symphony Enid was conducting.

There were running feet, then helping hands lifting her and dusting her off.

"I've just moved in," Enid was saying. "It's all a bit of a shambles and my children are so busy."

Kindly mothers helped her back to her kitchen table. Someone put the kettle on as Enid continued her tale of woe, the mother's faces darkening at the thoughtlessness of children.

Enid drank her tea in silence as the mothers tidied and organised and made phone calls.

The evening would be full of the smell of fresh paint and the sound of ladders sliding across the linoleum as their men mended shelves and hung curtains.

For now, with the violins in full swing, she delivered her first instrumental solo.

"You really must let me repay you, you've all been so very kind. I'll bake a cake. I think I've got the ingredients."

Her new helpers smiled and told her not to be silly. They checked the cupboards for flour and sugar and then, when they found them empty, went shopping for the nice old lady.

Beneath the kitchen table, Enid's hands gripped her walking stick and tapped out the time, one two three, one two three.

"Oh, yes!" she thought as her new orchestra scuttled to and fro.

"Oh, yes!"

Difficulty at the Beginning works supreme success, furthering through perseverance. Nothing should be undertaken. It furthers one to appoint helpers.

Youthful Folly

4. *Mêng*

I've been in the bookies all day: won one, lost three and I'm twenty quid down on the day.

My kid's outside, pressing his face on the glass, squinting at the telly; scribbling in his notebook, like always.

I go out for a smoke.

I say, "Alright, Kev."

"Alright," he says.

"Do us a favour, Dad," Kev says.

Here it comes, the same old question.

"Put a bet on for us?"

His book is full of losers, fractions of horses all over the place.

"Go on, then," I say. "Now get lost."

His money's in my hand; it smells like her, that perfume she likes, that little bottle she keeps in her bag.

Kev doesn't look me in the eye. He doesn't want to see that I already know.

Back inside, I don't place the bet, just stand there watching the telly and clock the horse come dead last.

This goes on; I take the money, the horse loses. Most of the cash pays Kev's child support and stops my ex from bitching. The rest comes with me down the pub.

"Don't worry," I say. "They'll figure it out eventually."

I wink at the barmaid, she knows the score.

She shakes her head, counts out my change in coppers, thinks I'm a bastard.

Youthful Folly has success. It is not I who seek the young fool; the young fool seeks me. If he asks two or three times, it is importunity. If he importunes, I give him no information. Perseverance furthers.

Waiting (Nourishment)

5. Hsu

She was always late, making deals, taking calls, waving him to silence, turning away before a touch.

Instead he did the housework, or so she thought. He used the money she left and hired a cleaner. He sat in the park, watched the clouds, read books and fed the pigeons with the last of his bagel.

He just wanted her to be happy. He was happy and he wished she'd just stop once in a while and feed the fucking pigeons.

The dinner was his idea. He'd put the date in her calendar under a client's name so he'd be sure she'd show up.

On the night itself, another anniversary she'd forgotten, he'd dressed in his best suit and the tie she'd bought him. He'd found it stuffed in her luggage and put it on while she flustered and told him she was glad he liked it.

He ordered for her and while he waited he filled his pockets with breadsticks for tomorrow's pigeons.

The main course arrived. He stared at the empty seats

and didn't even flinch when a hand landed on his shoulder, her parents arriving with her irritating brother.

He ordered more wine, glancing at her empty chair when father asked where she was and shrugged his shoulders. Then he took one of his fries, reached across the table and ground it into her avocado salad.

"Is everything all right?" her mother said and took his hand.

He frowned.

After all these years he'd completely forgotten how to answer the question.

Clouds rise up to heaven: The image of Waiting. Thus the superior man eats and drinks, is joyous and of good cheer. Three uninvited guests arrive. Honour them, and in the end there will be good fortune.

Conflict

6. Sung

Every Thursday Betty and Pauline from number twenty-three would queue up for their pensions and meet, eyeball to eyeball, to do battle in the charity shops.

You could set your watch by it and Betty did. She had that nice one her Anthony had brought back from holiday, with the brand name misspelt and a battery instead of a decent movement.

Betty saw Pauline cast her eyes over the figurines, the decorative plates and the jewellery display on the counter while she pretended to test the seams of an old checked shirt.

When Pauline moved over to the books Betty pounced, snatching a brooch from the counter and holding it up to the light. It glittered like sin and she put it back gently where anyone could see it, made a show of patting her pockets and went to find her purse.

The moment her back was turned the till rang. Betty turned. Pauline looked triumphant, the brooch already in her bag and then she was gone, slamming the door behind her.

Pauline's place was a house of treasures, gaudy but the real thing. Gold shone, emeralds cast their deep ocean light and the porcelain was so thin you could see her victorious smirk right through it.

After Pauline's husband had the cancer and then her boy had got his photo on the news in his smart uniform with a flag on his coffin, Betty and the others had found these gems and played the charity shop game when Pauline's pride had refused any other help.

She'll never want for anything again, Betty thought, as the Thursday battles raged. War is hell.

One cannot engage in conflict; one returns home, gives way. The people of this town, three hundred households, remain free of guilt.

The Army

7. *Shih*

We'd been in the Pit, the old limestone quarry at the back of the woods, just digging about with sticks and Danny's plastic spade and eating sweets, when Kenny found one.

He washed it off in the milky water and brought it over. When he put it down his finger was bleeding.

Pete poked it with a stick. It was a flint, the sharpest, knobbiest, pointiest, nastiest flint *ever*.

"Wow," said Danny and tapped it with his foot. "Got any more?"

"I'll give you the bag if you find any," said Pete. He was in charge. He was the oldest. He had the sweets.

That was the rest of the afternoon sorted. We broke some good sticks and got covered in white mud but we did it. A pile of them. Loads.

Pete chucked his bag at us. "Go on," he said.

We ate the lot. Too much liquorice.

Pete stared at the stones, put them in his bag.

"We can sort out Bobby's gang once and for all with these," he said.

We followed Pete up to the trees where our old camp

had been. Bobby and his lot were swinging on the rope.

Pete opened his bag. He gave us three stones each. We aimed.

"I *like* this game," said Pete.

Bobby was bigger than us. After his gang had run and he lay still in the mud we knew it wasn't over. The gang would come snivelling back with their mums and dads in tow.

But we'd be ready.

In the middle of the earth is water: The image of the Army. Thus the superior man increases his masses by generosity toward the people. There is game in the field. Let the eldest lead the army.

Holding Together (Union)

8. *Pī*

Sitting with their crews in the back bar of The Trawlerman, hunched over their pints, are Colin, Captain of The Merry, with arms like old rope and Tom, Captain of the Argus, his cable-knit jumper as salt-hardened as armour.

They pass the occasional word to other fishermen, but a silence stretches between these two men like an empty net.

In the harbour their boats are moored side-by-side, their gear is entangled in a great knot of chain and nylon for which neither man will admit fault and for which neither man will pay.

Into the bar walks a tiny woman, her face like leather, eyes straight from the coals in the hearth. She walks to the middle of the room, refusing any offers of drink.

"Boys," she says.

Colin and Tom stare at their mother.

"Are you going to let these other lads get back to work?" she asks.

Silence.

"Whose table are you keeping food from?" she asks.

"Yours, Mum," they say.

She nodded.

"You know what to do," she said.

And the two great men got up from their seats, knelt in front of their mother and bowed their heads.

You hear it said, but I'd never seen it done for real.

Her hands whipped forward and grabbed an ear apiece and then she pulled hard and knocked their bloody heads together.

Afterwards the brothers went down to the dock and cut the chains and nylon that bound their boats. Then, with their crews where they belonged, they set off to sail alone, always together on the sea.

Holding Together brings good fortune. Inquire of the oracle once again. Thus the kings of antiquity bestowed the different states as fiefs and cultivated friendly relations with the feudal lords.

The Taming Power of the Small

9. *Hsiao Ch'u*

Just before midnight the rain comes, beating on the skylights and washing the dust from the gutters. The moon, still swelling, is pinned inches over the horizon far from the edge of the storm.

"We can't child-proof, that's the problem," she says waving her wine glass at the steel framed furniture, the unbroken surfaces of pale concrete.

She isn't even pregnant, he thinks, and runs his fingers over soft leather. Three months together and she's already talking about kids.

She won't last long; they never do after the kid conversation.

They look at each other briefly then look away, each finding some small detail in the room to focus on.

He pours brandy into lead crystal, takes a breath, feels the weight.

"And where did this new sofa come from?" she asks.

Somewhere to sit is suddenly more important than imaginary nappies.

He raises his eyebrows, non-committal.

"It's all so artificial," she says.

"Leather, cotton, stone, what's artificial about that?" he asks.

"It's just so impersonal, too much design."

The skin on her arms is so smooth, so white.

"Like couture?" he asks.

She is plucked and preened, toned and moisturised, flat beauty from a magazine.

He strokes the leather sofa, thinks about smooth, white cushions and the silence that will come from this small decision.

Just as before, he is very calm.

Dense clouds, no rain from our western region. The wind drives across heaven: Man and wife roll their eyes. If you are sincere, blood vanishes and fear gives way. Perseverance brings the woman into danger. The moon is nearly full. If the superior man persists, misfortune comes.

Treading (Conduct)

10. *Lu*

There was a hole in the garden. It ruined the view of the trees and hung there, the size of a manhole cover on its edge, five feet above the ground.

Felicity peered at it through the kitchen window then put her boots on.

A closer look did not improve matters. She prodded it with a length of cane she'd been using for the runner beans but the tip just vanished, faded away into the darkness.

Felicity inched closer and peered around the edge. She could make out some kind of shape in the darkness, maybe a tree, it was difficult to tell.

She thought about the hole while she was weeding, thought about it while she deadheaded the roses and put her peelings in a bucket for the compost heap. Then, as she trudged up the garden, she stopped, looked left and right to see if the neighbours were watching, and emptied the bucket into the hole, weeds and all.

She told her husband, who frowned like always. He stood and smoked his pipe and traced the edge of the circle while she demanded, "Well? What are you going to do about it?" over and over again.

"A bucket of weeds?" he asked.

"Yes, right through," she said with her hands on her hips.

He lifted her easily, his arms around her shoulders and hips. She fell onto a soft pile of leaves and old potato peelings.

"Geoffrey!" she was shouting. "Geoffrey!"

She felt the hot night air, smelled the musk and heard the animal sounds amongst the trees, saw the branches moving, something black and orange approaching.

"Geoffrey!"

She looked up, searching for the hole. There, instead, was the bright full moon with the faintest hint of a smile.

.

He treads on the tail of the tiger. The tiger bites the man. Look to your conduct and weigh the favourable signs. When everything is fulfilled, supreme good fortune comes.

Peace

11. *T'ai*

A new city. She'd loaded the car and left before he'd made it home and told no one. She was uprooted, standing in the sunshine in front of a Cathedral looking in the paper for rooms to rent, looking for somewhere to unload what little history she'd brought with her.

She found somewhere to drink and bought a tall orange juice with plenty of ice and sat outside, out of sight of the dartboard.

"I'll drink my bloody poof's drink if I want and you can stuff your half of lager," she thought.

A hundred a week, en suite shower, no bills, own key.

The bookstore knew of course. They'd helped her transfer, found a spot in a shop far away. The HR woman nearly cried, but didn't.

Hundred and ten, large sunny room. Lockable door.

The day was seeping into her bones, easing her aches and pains from so many boxes, the hours of driving.

People in the street kept walking past, not spying for him, just getting lunch, playing guitar, juggling.

Ninety a week, double bed, new mattress. Private entrance.

A well-dressed man at the next table was being friendly. She talked to him, told him a little, asked where places were.

"You don't want to live there," he said pointing. "It's a bit common."

"I don't mind," she said, but crosses it off anyway.

"I'll leave you alone to call," he said, shook his empty glass and wandered inside. She smiled at the back over his jacket. He's more her age.

A hundred quid a week and not having to share it, or do the washing up, or iron your old checked shirts, or anything else in the night.

She sat in silence and sunlight, centred and still. Happy.

Her phone rang; she saw her mother's name and smashed it on the floor and kept stamping on the plastic as the lunchtime crowd looked on.

The small departs, the great approaches. When ribbon grass is pulled up, the sod comes with it. Bearing with the uncultured in gentleness, Fording the river with resolution, Not neglecting what is distant, Not regarding one's companions: Thus one may manage to walk in the middle.

Standstill (Stagnation)

12. *P'i*

Jules is waiting at the bus station: stripy shirt, pinstripe trousers and no braces. His coat is at home with the endless dust.

The woman from the job centre had used her sympathetic voice, shook her head, then signed off this week's redundancy insurance for the home he has to sell, the house that echoes only with his footsteps since his wife left him and took all the rugs.

"Vehicles, derivatives and futures," he lists the tools of finance in his head. "Useless then, less than useless now." The newspaper headlines are a mirror of his gloom.

The estate agent calls. Good news or bad depending on how you look at it. The sale has broken even, paid off the mortgage but not a single penny more.

"There must be something I can do," he thinks.

He'd left school at sixteen with no qualifications, just like his heroes, and he'd bragged about it. He'd got into trading on his own, then a small firm, then the big bank. It was all champagne after that, the car, the girl, the heated indoor pool. Then this.

He lists his skills and knows most of them mean nothing in the real world. What else can he do? Putting up a shelf is a poor cousin of carpentry, wiring a plug doesn't make him an electrician.

A bus pulls up and an old woman struggles with her shopping and Jules offers a hand, helps her slowly to her seat and wonders how many oranges one person really needs.

He breathes in the smell of the seats, feels the satisfying vibration of the engine, reassuring joys from a childhood almost forgotten.

Jules steps off the bus and marches over to the station manager's office, opens his wallet and slaps his driver's licence on the counter.

"Vehicles," he thinks and asks for an application form.

Heaven and earth do not unite: The image of Standstill. Thus the superior man falls back upon his inner worth in order to escape the difficulties. He does not permit himself to be honoured with revenue.

Fellowship with Men

13. *T'ung Jên*

David had been looking forward to Saturday all week but caught a paintball in the throat five minutes into the game and lay there, face down in the earth, gasping while he listened to the laughter.

The Blues, out-of-towners who had shown up in their battered pickup trucks with their own guns and armour, were standing around sniggering as the medic came running over.

"I'm gonna die here," David thought, and blacked out.

When he woke up in hospital the guys had all brought him flowers.

The next week he went to find The Blues, to look them in the eye. He walked right into their bar and showed off the greens and yellows the bruise had become. He joined in with the back-slapping and the fag-hating, good-old-boy bullshit and played along, refused to buy a stolen car, wrote their real names on the rematch sheet and promised them steaks and no hard feelings.

The rest of his team grumbled and gave him disapproving looks. It was consorting with the enemy, they said, a betrayal of the unspoken rules.

David phoned the police, told them about the stolen car, and bought the steaks for Saturday.

The Blues thundered in to the car park, hanging off the sides of the pickup, guns at the ready.

The police were waiting, two cruisers and a puncture strip to slow them down a little. The Blues, each one of them a suspected car thief, were swiftly cuffed and taken away, except one, who ran and nearly made it across the field before a taser took him to the ground.

David took their paint guns. Leaned in through the police cruiser's window and blew a kiss at the unsmiling officer.

David wanted the team to be called The Pinks after that. There was no argument.

Fellowship with Men in the open, Success. Men bound in fellowship first weep and lament, But afterward they laugh. After great struggles they succeed in meeting. No remorse.

Possession in Great Measure

14. *Ta Yu*

The truck stop was filling up. Under cover of night the great rigs were rolling off the interstate and into the sulphurous glare of the arc lights over the gas station forecourt. Tired, sweaty men moved with grizzly purpose towards the diner, their huge hands scratching their bellies into silence.

Carl waited by his rig until the others had gone on ahead.

"Hey baby," he said wiping the bugs from the warm chrome. "There's my girl, pretty as anything."

From the depths of the truck came a slow, pneumatic hiss.

"I know honey," Carl said and buffed some paintwork. "But I need to eat and I'm sure you need something."

There was a brief snort of hot air as the suspension came to rest under her new weight.

"I'll be sure to get you something nice," he said.

The diner was half empty. Truckers sat hunched over their food, eating fast before they fell asleep.

A new kid was loading up with scrambled eggs and steak.

"You're Brody's kid, ain'tcha?" Carl asked. "How is he?"

"He's with Jesus. It's a blessing after his illness. I'm Hooper."

Carl finished eating first. He had something to say.

"Do you own your rig?" he asked.

"Nope. It'll be years before I'll have that kind of cash."

"Let's play cards," Carl said. "Maybe you can win some."

Carl played to lose and handed over the truck's paperwork.

Hooper stared at his good luck. "What's she carrying?"

Carl wiped his hands on his oil stained jeans, thought about his whispered promises in the night, the one he'd just broken.

"Too early to tell," he said. "Give it a few months."

He was too old for her anyway.

No relationship with what is harmful; There is no blame in this. If one remains conscious of difficulty, one remains without blame. A big wagon for loading. A Prince offers it to the Son of Heaven. A petty man cannot do this.

Modesty

15. *Ch'ien*

He'd been published in the Seventies, won prizes, been fêted and then forgotten. His book had eventually gone out of print, fallen out of favour, until even its title had disappeared.

At least the hardware store was a steady job. In many ways he preferred it to writing, it was more concrete, another way of building things, less ephemeral.

He liked to sand wood, smooth off the edges, make one piece flow into the next after he slotted them together. He built and did not write and was satisfied.

The arty lot would pop in once in a while and ask him to speak. He never went over the river. He preferred the old town and hated bars.

They'd ask him once a month, trying to get the local prize-winner to talk about the process, the struggle, the insomnia. They hadn't read his book, they just knew about the prize. The book itself had become a mythic thing, abstract, unnecessary for their purposes.

He always said he was working on something new, refining a few pieces that he would share one day, just not anytime soon.

But they pestered him and flattered him while he thought about wood and nails and glue.

So one day he agreed. He asked what they were expecting and they, caught out by the unexpected yes, said anything, anything would do. Tell us what you've learned from being a writer.

He retreated into his workshop and finished what he'd started.

On the night itself he caught the train. The river passed below him, mighty, ever changing and anonymous, flowing like the grain of mahogany.

On stage he was asked to speak and instead whipped back the sheet the deliverymen had draped over his new work, a handmade desk and chair made with as much harmony and skill as any of his words.

"This is what I've learned," he said. "When you write you've got to be comfortable."

The other writers came and sat, and knew that he was right.

A superior man modest about his modesty may cross the great water. He weighs things and makes them equal.

Enthusiasm

16. *Yu*

After church everyone went over to Benny's. The chrome on their bikes gleamed with the summer sun, their handle -bars sticky and close to melting and their backpacks full of comics, warm orange juice, and bubble-gum turned to fruity glue.

Benny went to the garage for ice. The great double doors slid upward and he held onto the pull-rope letting it lift him off his feet.

"All right?" Jeff asked as his friends came to find him.

Pauley and Dunc were staring around the walls in the cool garage air.

"What is all this stuff?" Dunc asked. "Is this your Dad's? From when he was in a band?"

Pauley pulled out a record, still in its plastic. "What's this?" he asked.

"It's a record. You know. Before CDs," Benny said.

"*Judgement*, by the Ancient Kings," Pauley said turning it over and over. "Metal. Nice."

"Christian metal," Benny said quickly and handed out the ice.

"How long were they going?" Dunc asked as he wandered down the shelves past the posters and guitars.

"Coming up forty years," Benny said. "Seventy three 'til now."

"He still plays? Pretty full on for an old guy," Pauley said.

Dunc was looking at the band photo. "Does he look the same, your dad, in the photo I mean?"

"Not really," Benny said. "His hair's shorter."

Forty years of music, like an endless prayer, had certainly worked its wonders to behold.

It was true, his hair was shorter but the pain in his hands was worse from playing with small fingers. It was worth it.

"Praise Him," Benny thought. "Hallelujah!"

Thus the ancient kings made music in order to honour merit and offered it with splendour to the Supreme Deity, inviting their ancestors to be present.

Following

17. *Sui*

The swimming pool was always crowded in the holidays; endless pink bodies ploughed up and down in the lanes, children in the shallow end in orange armbands splashing around, the deep end full of divers and the swimming certificate lifesaving class.

Maureen just wanted to float, to lie there and let her body relax and hear the echoes of voices, muffled and booming underwater.

She slipped into the pool, her slight frame moving gracefully into the middle.

She closed her eyes and listened to the soft explosions of people plunging in like far away thunder.

The Red Sea had been the best place; her body had lain on top of the salt water while the sun baked her fragile limbs. She'd never been so comfortable.

Her husband had never gone swimming; he'd hated it, never even rolled his trousers up. He'd sat on the beach and stared at the shops and the candyfloss stalls instead of the view.

She'd spent the war listening to the radio in a hut in

Milton Keynes and hadn't met Anthony until he'd surfaced when it was all over.

On their honeymoon in Spain he'd closed their curtains against the sea and sat out of the way to smoke amongst the plumbing and empty beer crates.

For a man in the navy she'd always found this a little odd.

But the ocean had taken a grip on him below the North Atlantic, no more than a boy, encased in a submarine while all around him the war had thundered on the other side of the hull.

She'd scattered her husband's ashes on a mountain in the rain. One day they'll reach the sea, she thought, and the deep would welcome him as one of its own, its voice booming underwater.

Thunder in the middle of the lake: The image of Following. If one clings to the little boy, one loses the strong man. If one clings to the strong man, one loses the little boy.

Work on What Has Been Spoiled (Decay)

18. *Ku*

The bloody car sits there on its blocks like the stupid, ambitious, unfinished project it really was.

Mum never wanted to move it, wanted me to go over and spend my Sundays in grease and frustration, making the familiar noises that would let her think he was still... but he isn't and I wouldn't.

Now she's gone and I miss the sound of her washing up and her talking to the radio more than my Dad's clanking and swearing.

The broken plate is still in the sink from her stroke. It came on so quickly she didn't have time to take her rubber gloves off. The tap was left running after they'd taken her away.

I will ignore the car for now, that can wait.

Her clothes go into bin bags, her books into boxes. I keep some old favourites: *The Old Curiosity Shop*, *Paradise Lost*. There isn't much, it only takes an afternoon. The removal men will come for the rest. They'll try and sell it for me but there's no money in furniture.

I drink black coffee, two sugars. No milk, the fridge is empty.

The garage is full of tools. I wouldn't know where to begin.

There's the sheet, still on the table, every cog and spring laid out in neat rows. I can't read my Dad's handwriting. No instructions, not like Lego.

Here's the superglue on the shelf next to the spanners and the extra sparkplugs.

I sit on the kitchen floor to mend the broken plate and cut myself on a sharp edge.

And then the tears come.

Setting right what has been spoiled by the father. If there is a son, no blame rests upon the departed father. Danger. In the end good fortune.

Approach

19. *Lin*

Mr Harris sold encyclopaedias door to door, pulled the trolley behind his tweeds and brogues, and counted the number of times his salesman's knock had been answered in the last month; how many times they saw him coming and hid behind their sofas.

But not Ms Neville, oh no. Every time he called at number 32 the old woman herded him into the kitchen with her stick and sat him down for tea and cake.

She was already up to "HIL to KIN" and was always happy to rummage in her purse for the pounds it took to buy another.

Her cake was getting better too, moist and delicious.

"It's hard to get out these days," she said as she shuffled over to the cupboard. "I'm glad for the company. I like learning about you, about the world."

When she asked what delights were in store this time he always felt like a teacher, suddenly much older.

Month after month and soon she was up to "REL to YUN". She opened it with her paper hands and offered him tea from the pot and another slice.

When he called again the door was already open. She called down stairs for him to wait in the kitchen.

Pinned to the wall were delicate pages, the page for Tea another for Cake, a third for Dancing.

On the stairs he heard the lightest of footsteps.

Here, pinned above the kettle, the page for Youth.

Approach has supreme success. Perseverance furthers. Thus the superior man is inexhaustible in his will to teach.

Contemplation (View)

20. *Kuan*

The village was nothing more than mud huts and woven lean-tos squatting in the sun, the villagers huddled in the doorways.

The truck lurched to a stop. Jenny, Ed and the rest unloaded the gear while Derek asked the questions.

"Where is the leader?" he managed in the local dialect.

Derek showed the thin chieftain their equipment, explained about the well and the pump they were here to install. The chief shrugged and told them they could do what they wanted.

Derek was in his element. "Did you ever have Meccano when you were a kid?" he asked Jenny.

"Nintendo," Jenny said.

"That's why I love it," Derek said ignoring her. "It's just like playing at building cranes."

"This is people's lives we are talking about," Ed said.

"I know. Can't I enjoy myself?"

Derek directed the construction and shooed away the village children until everyone was tired of his voice and he was left alone to give everything a final check.

He pushed the pump handle, heard a hiss but nothing happened.

He fiddled with the pipework but still nothing. The frustration overwhelmed him. He ran his finger over the plans.

"Where's the non-return valve?" he shouted. "Oh, here it is!"

He tightened the nut and set to the handle, the pipe glopped and hissed and then gushed black oil onto the parched earth.

"Well that's not supposed to happen!" he said as the villagers danced and whooped and shook his hand.

"Now we *buy* water!" shouted the chief. "Get a swimming pool! A Ferrari!"

"What have you done!?" Ed was shouting. "What have you done!?"

Derek considered the beautiful grassland, the herd of antelope in the distance, the crystal blue sky, and sighed.

The wind blows over the earth: The image of Contemplation. Thus the kings of old visited the regions of the world, contemplated the people, and gave them instruction. Boy-like contemplation. For an inferior man, no blame, for a superior man, humiliation.

Biting Through

21. *Shih Ho*

Carla hated prison food. She looked despondently at her plate: brown, runny, green, yellow, cold. These were the adjectives of incarceration.

Sitting at the end of their usual bench Frankie immediately started nagging Carla to give up her pudding, the lardy cow.

Carla picked at the frayed edges of her denims, pushed food around with her fork, ate enough to stop her from fainting in the yard and traded her unwanted chips for cigarettes.

She tightened her belt another notch, trapping the hunger in thick leather, and chewed the gristly meat, whatever it was.

She palmed her fork up her sleeve. The saltshaker vanished into a pocket.

"What are you in here for?" a new girl asked.

"Nothing," Carla said. "Mind your business."

"She's in here for muurderrrrr," Fat Frankie said wobbling her big arms about.

"Your daughter starved to death, wasn't it?" another

woman butted in. There was silence at the table.

"Made her do some celebrity diet, yeah? She was a bit pudgy, right?" said a third.

"You're only a kid yourself, look at you," Frankie said.

Carla was twenty-five, her daughter had been eight years old.

Everyone was staring and Frankie was laughing, her mouth wide, the gaps in her teeth full of stolen food.

Carla wanted to be sick. She left her tray and ran.

In her cell she drank all the salt in a mug of water and was ill into the sink for hours.

She scratched her weight on the wall with the fork, a smaller number every day.

Soon she would lose the weight of her guilt: enough to make a little girl.

Biting Through has success. It is favourable to let justice be administered. Thus the kings of former times made firm the laws through clearly defined penalties. Bites on old dried meat and strikes on something poisonous.

Grace

22. Pì

After Girl Guides the four of them were outside waiting to go home. Emily, Claire and Jodie had been counting up the cookies they'd sold but skinny, perfect Charlotte was winning.

"My daddy sells them at his work!" she shouted. "He's very important! He tells them that if they don't buy them all they'll be in trouble!"

A group of bearded men were queuing for soup across the street, some of them stared.

The other girls had seen Charlotte's daddy pick her up in his big red car. He must be important. Their daddies only had little cars.

Emily had been up and down her street and knocked on every door. She'd sold eight boxes and she'd done it herself and she said so.

Charlotte looked sulky for a second. "But I'm still going to win!" she hissed and stormed off.

Claire hadn't sold any yet. She was shy and didn't like knocking on doors. Doors had strangers behind them.

Jodie had given her cookies to her mum to sell to her

friends. Mummy's friends were lovely and always helped.

Then the cars arrived.

Skinny Charlotte slammed her door and the others could see her daddy shouting as he drove away.

Claire's mummy made a big fuss of her being outside near all these strange men across the street.

When Jodie's mum appeared she said sorry, her friends were all on diets. The boxes were in the boot.

Jodie knew it didn't really matter if she won, so she took an armful of boxes and carefully crossed the road and put them on the soup table.

"Keep them," she said to the soup lady.

All the beardy men said thank you and Jodie smiled all the way home.

But, even though she said she'd given all of her cookies away, she'd really kept some of the boxes in her room. Then she gave them all to skinny, perfect Charlotte, who ate and ate and ate.

Grace has success. In small matters it is favourable to undertake something. Constant perseverance brings good fortune. Humiliation, but in the end good fortune. Simple grace. No blame.

Splitting Apart

23. Po

When they broke down the door, the neighbours peered around the policemen's shoulders to see Harry Talbot's body: an old man in his dressing gown and slippers, a broken mug of tea flung against the radiator, all life departed.

The ambulance came and went, photographers snapped, investigators measured, social workers shook their heads and shut the door behind them.

They took the body, but left Harry Talbot.

The stairs were where he had expected them to be; a hole in the living room floor, heat rising from the depths, red lit and curving away out of sight.

One foot followed another as he felt the terrible weight of the bargain he had made all those years ago and headed down.

Down into the light.

Above, The Mountain. Below, The Earth. Splitting Apart. It does not further one to go anywhere. Thus those above can ensure their position only by giving generously to those below.

Return (The Turning Point)

24. *Fu*

It had all started when she came back from the shops on Tuesday. There were Tom and the children, smiling at her in the living room, like nothing had happened.

She phoned her friends who tried to reassure her, to calm her down, to understand what the hell she was ranting on about.

Her mum said "Claire, don't worry, love." So, of course, Claire worried.

They were there the next day and the day after that. Every time she came home, smile, smile, smile. It was unbearable.

The next week she had a business trip. Seven days living out of a suitcase in Edinburgh. She felt calmer, didn't have to walk around her own living room with her eyes shut.

On Thursday Tom phoned. She could hear the children in the background.

"Are you all right?" he asked. "Your mum rang me. She said you were…"

"Are you smiling?" she shouted. "Are you smiling right now!?"

She slammed the phone down and sat fully clothed in the shower eating wine gums until she felt better.

On the way home she started to shake. In the airport lounge she had two large gins, then two more in a wine bar after she landed.

It took her half an hour to open her front door. Some of her friends arrived; they'd arranged to meet, to help poor Claire.

She stood in the living room doorway and opened her eyes. The three smiles were there, bright eyed, happy, distant.

She screamed for so long her breath became no more than rattles over her dry tongue. She clawed at the carpet, kicked her suitcase, tore at her clothes. Her friends called an ambulance. The paramedics injected a sedative and took her away.

Claire's friends tidied up before they left.

"It's bad enough he divorced her," one said, "so why keep the photographs?"

Friends come without blame. Return from a short distance. No need for remorse. Repeated return. Danger. Walking in the midst of others, one returns alone. Misfortune from within and without.

Innocence (The Unexpected)

25. *Wu Wang*

They wandered into the bar, leather jackets, shaved heads and made a beeline for my spot.

"You Trevor?" one asked.

"What of it?" I replied.

We all sat in a corner booth. Spanners and Jack their names were. We talked business.

"So, We'll be out of there in eight minutes. You'll be out front in the car, engine running. Got it?" says Spanners.

"And it's tomorrow. Queen's Jubilee," Jack said.

We stayed for another drink, and another, then shorts. I woke up with a hangover and an envelope full of cash stuffed down my trousers.

Jack came and got me and took me to the garage. In the darkness ranks of fast, old cars were being repaired and re-sprayed.

I drove an old Jaguar into town and parked outside the BBC. My head was pounding and there, just across the road, was a pharmacy.

I left the engine running. It's not like I'm doing anything wrong.

Two aspirin and a bottle of water and I'm out on the pavement and the car is gone. I see it vanish around the corner, hear the stereo up loud.

Jack and Spanners are in the doorway. Between them is that blousy, red-headed duchess who got divorced from Prince whatsit. They're shouting at me – something about the palace.

I leg it, figuring that they won't leave the royal on her own. I make it down the tube and go back to my mum's to lie low.

It's all part of this getting people off the dole thing. I did time for driving other people's cars when I shouldn't have, so the woman at the benefit office sets my up with this!

I'll never live it down if it gets out. Driving for the bloody cops!

Mum turns on the telly, hears that whatshername isn't there. The news woman uses the word 'snub'.

"It's a shame how they treated her," she says and waves her little flag.

If someone is not as he should be, he has misfortune, and it does not further him to undertake anything. The cow that was tethered by someone is the wanderer's gain, the citizen's loss. Use no medicine in an illness incurred through no fault of your own, it will pass of itself.

The Taming Power of the Great

26. Ta Ch'u

Keith sat in the café and unwrapped his sandwich. The thick tomato sauce was already on his trousers and, after a brief wipe, was all over his jumper too.

He cursed librarians everywhere, opened his bag and stacked the books in front of him: *The Way of the Warrior*, *The Art of War*, *The Book of Five Rings*, *The Worst-Case Scenario Survival Handbook*. Quite a collection, but these were desperate times and he had to do something.

Keith read up about mugging, his least favourite topic. Then he read about how to slice an opponent with the tip of your sword. It made him feel better.

Outside, the lunchtime crowd were gathering and, standing amongst them, three green jumpers with name tags and polyester trousers all the same. Their leader, "Anthony – Non-Fiction", was standing with "Bob – History" and "Trevor – Biography". They were smoking and watching the tourists, the kids, anyone who had just come out of the bookshop across the street.

"Unemployed louts," Keith thought and practised his dragon claw.

He read more about lightning blows to the windpipe, imagined the sound of a crushed larynx, all the while glancing at the window.

They were still there. He had another double espresso, felt the caffeine fire him up, felt the words of Bushido rise off the page and put fire in his veins.

Leaving the café and being punched in the face wasn't part of the plan.

The gang took the books gently from his bag while Trevor – Biography - kept a foot on his chest.

"Why?" Keith asked the librarians. "Why do you do it?"

"We're not stealing them," Anthony - Non-Fiction - said. "It's the budget cuts. The library closures, you know. Call it a loan." The others laughed on cue and kicked him again.

The Way of the Warrior parted company with Keith.

Not eating at home brings good fortune. Thus the superior man acquaints himself with many sayings of antiquity and many deeds of the past, in order to strengthen his character thereby. Danger is at hand. It furthers one to desist.

The Corners of the Mouth

27. *Yi*

My host pushed his chair back from the dining table, his blotchy hands roaming across his belly like crabs inspecting the carcass of a whale. He shifted uncomfortably, sliding his misshapen bulk against the seatback before settling, legs splayed, to stare at me over the cheeseboard.

He gaze was aristocratic indifference but his fingers, tapping on the tablecloth, belied his calm.

"The mountain, you say?" he asked.

I nodded. Through the window the view stretched across the jungle to the dark massif beyond.

The old man leaned forward. "Was it difficult to find?"

I spread a map on the table and showed him the route, told him about the whispers and rumours that had led us onwards and the spot amongst the cliffs that had delivered our prize.

He wiped his mouth with his napkin.

"I would shake you by the hand," he said, "but I'm afraid that if I did…" He let the words fade away as he scratched a flaking patch of skin.

In front of him the Wedgewood bowl sat empty, the silver spoon tarnishing quickly in the remnants of his thin meal.

"Can you be sure of its authenticity?" he asked. For the first time I heard something desperate and hopeful in his voice.

On the white linen his hands had ceased their endless scratching, the skin whitening as blisters calmed and faded.

I reached into the bag beside my chair and lifted the reliquary onto the table. The faded cushion it contained was empty.

He reached forward but he caught sight of his fingers, newly slim and clear of his affliction. He touched his face in wonder.

"My God," he gasped and crossed himself.

The true relic stayed hidden in my pack, bound for a museum. The object I had given this man's cook had come from a street hawker, a peddler of saintly bones left over from his lunch.

My host licked the spoon and then the bowl, his harsh tongue lapping up every drop.

The power of his belief was a thing to behold.

Once, when I was small, I'd had the measles and had asked God to stop the spots.

"Pray? Pray all you like," my mother said, "but promise me you'll eat your chicken soup."

Pay heed to the providing of nourishment and to what a man seeks to fill his own mouth with. Turning to the summit for provision of nourishment brings good fortune.

Preponderance of the Great

28. *Ta Kuo*

I thought he'd been in the river for a year, down amongst the roots and tumbling stones.

My mother told me otherwise.

On a bookshelf something remained.

She'd taken it from the crematorium, she said, and he's as useful around the house now as he ever was alive.

I wondered about the jar of grey ashes, which bit of him hadn't made it to the river: an ear, a nose, the hand that clenched his pipe?

Incomplete, my father flows away, and somewhere a fisherman eats his catch, picks grit from his teeth and thinks, inexplicably, about tobacco.

The lake rises above the trees: Thus the superior man, when he stands alone, is unconcerned, and if he has to renounce the world, he is undaunted. One must go through the water. It goes over one's head. Misfortune. No blame.

The Abysmal (Water)

29. *K'an*

Afterwards, Margaret sat in the living room. She tried to read a magazine and cried a little at the unfairness of it all. Worse than losing her job, her livelihood, were her imagined prospects of finding another.

Her sixty-three year old reflection wouldn't meet her eye in the in the mirror in the downstairs loo.

"You don't look very confident, whoever you are," she thought.

The car sat in the driveway, weeds in the grille, crumpled and immobile.

In the dilapidated shed at the bottom of the garden she re-arranged the faded magazines, drank a bottle of wine and waited for her husband to get home.

Graham stood at the end of the lawn and smoked his pipe in silence. She told him everything through the broken window and refused to come out, although he never asked.

Later she found a cup of tea cold on the gravel as if he'd forgotten to give it to her.

She slept in her clothes on some old garden furniture,

ignored the wind and the hedgehog scratching around the crooked door.

The next day she opened a box and found some forgotten knitting and made a glove with six fingers as she stared at the empty garden and found solace shut in between her thorn-hedged prison walls.

In the night there were more insistent hedgehog sounds and the wind picked and rattled the plastic bag she'd taped over the broken glass.

She knitted a scarf and then a hat and wore them with a fierce determination.

Making a jumper took rather longer. She knitted as many rows as she could from each ball then rummaged until she found more in another box and forged on, one small task at a time, until it was past her knees in great bright stripes of colour, the wool from her first cardigan, her sister's baby shoes, her husband's socks.

And all the while the wind pulled at the window, the animal noises became a determined scratching but she was comfortable in her bent wheelbarrow seat and her bed deep amongst the sackcloth and potatoes.

She wore the jumper and waited for the wind to stir the shingles and for the little claws to burrow at the rotten wood.

At last, clothed in the wool of memories, she put down her knitting needles and opened the door to let the darkness find her.

The abyss is dangerous. One should strive to attain small things only. Earthen vessels simply handed in through the window. The abyss is not filled to overflowing; it is filled only to the rim. Bound with cords and ropes, shut in between thorn-hedged prison walls: For three years one does not find the way. Misfortune.

The Clinging Fire

30. *Li*

They built an arch on the moon and called it Tranquility, a great machine full of fuel and people and determination, a monument to exploration that glittered in the light of the distant sun.

Beneath it was the rocket.

Ten thousand tons of steel and crackling ice stood embraced in endless sensors and restraints, waiting for the people from earth who would be the first to step onto another world.

Collins stood in the crater and bounced gently on her heels in her airtight shoes. She adjusted her visor and took a photograph, imagining the leap into space, the worlds of the old president urging her onwards; "Not because it is easy, but because it is hard."

Her great grandfather had waited in the capsule as Armstrong and Aldrin had walked in the dust and collected rocks, but she would be Captain, chosen after generations to be the first to walk on Mars.

She remembered sitting on her father's knee, her picture books like no other little girls. "'R' is for Rocket", he would tell her and stroke her hair, "and 'S' is for Space."

And in the back of his car, every time they'd passed the fast food place two blocks down from their house he'd ask, "And what is 'M' for, my darling girl?" and she'd shout the answer over and over. "Mars! Mars! Mars!"

She'd kept the book. It was the only personal thing she'd been allowed to take, for the children she'd never have, for the history she'd make, for the past generations who'd journey with her and for those who would follow.

When the Martian landscape appeared in the window of the rocket she saw the plains of dust and rust, the ice caps, the canals and the endless mountains.

"It's the Outback," she thought, "the Atacama desert, the Arctic, Everest. We've been here before, beaten these landscapes and survived worse."

With her father's picture book tucked beside her seat, she knew we'd be just fine.

For Ray Bradbury and Neil Armstrong
who passed away in 2012.

That which is bright rises twice: the image of Fire. Thus the great man, by perpetuating this brightness, illumines the four quarters of the world.

Influence (Wooing)

31. *Hsien*

John and Jack and Paul were huddled in a corner when Nurse Helen came in with her metal tray of pills.

"Hello, Gary," she said and smiled.

"Kill her," John said.

"Hey there, gorgeous," said Jack.

"Stop looking at me!" wailed Paul.

"Shut up!" Gary shouted.

The nurse shook her head and put some pills into a cup.

"Are you going to take these nicely," she asked, "or am I going to have to make you?"

"Poison," John hissed.

"Yes," Gary said. "I'll take them."

The nurse put the cup on the table and took a step back.

Gary tipped them out and lined them up in a neat row before swallowing each with a small sip of water.

"I can feel them working," Jack said, closing his eyes and smiling. "It feels good."

"Stick your fingers down your throat, puke them up!" John demanded.

The door opened and Doctor Matthews took in the

scene, Gary swallowing the buttons from his pyjamas, the empty glass, the hand that clutched at the torn bedclothes.

"He's not a real doctor," Nurse Helen said.

"He'll kill us all," John warned.

"He wants to know where you live, then go to your house and see your wife and…" Jack interrupted.

"Shut up!" Gary shouted. "Please, shut up!"

"Who are you talking to?" Doctor Matthews asked, looking at the empty room. "Anyway, how are you finding your new place off the ward, do you like it?"

"They're still here, all of them. And now there's something worse."

"What's that?"

"Now there's you."

Behind Doctor Matthews the door opened and Mark, Gary's analyst stepped in. He smiled and opened his notebook before pulling up a chair.

"Now there's who?" Mark asked.

"The doctor," Gary replied.

"What doctor?"

Gary was on his feet, the chair in his hands.

"You're just another one, aren't you? No one's coming. No one will help me!"

Gary took a swing then looked down at the silent, bleeding figure on the floor.

"Well, that's never happened before," Nurse Helen said.

"Maybe you're getting better," they all said.

Perseverance brings good fortune. Remorse disappears. If a man is agitated in mind, And his thoughts go hither and thither. Only those friends on whom he fixes his conscious thoughts will follow.

Duration

32. *Hêng*

Upstairs at the motel he waits. The August heat melts the glue beneath the carpet tiles and the ceiling fan turns slowly through the thick, yellow afternoon.

He picks a broken nail against the polyester sheet, unravelling the hours with the loosening of thread, measuring days and weeks with the hundred dollar bills he slides beneath the door when the manager comes to croak his demands and thump his fist against the weathered paint, just once.

Four hundred dollars doesn't seem like long enough.

Through the bathroom window he can see the abandoned baseball diamond, white lines, heat shimmered, where the faintest movement in the air raises fine dust that settles in quiet strata on the parked cars.

Five hundred dollars comes and goes without sirens. There is no pounding on the door, no insistent calling of his name through a megaphone from the street below, just the scratching of his nails and the turning of the fan.

He rationalizes and justifies, deludes and distances himself from what he did five hundred dollars worth of

Tuesdays ago, the remainder of his conscience drowning in the heat of August.

Halfway through six hundred the eastern skies darken, great clouds gather and roll their thunderous guts over the sun.

Soon fat rain starts to fall, exploding in the diamond's dust, boiling over truck metal, steaming from rust hubcaps and pounding on the door.

He'd hoped these hundreds would have been long enough. But the car he'd abandoned on that Tuesday has been washed clean for curious eyes to see inside, the blanket on the back seat, the single red shoe.

The rain hammers on the door louder than any fist and quicker than a broken nail, it does not know or ask his name, pretends deafness to his pleas of innocence and washes his sins ready for the sun.

It won't be long now.

Thunder and wind: the image of Duration. Remorse disappears. No game in the field. Restlessness as an enduring condition brings misfortune.

Retreat

33. Tun

It was a rout. The defeated cavalry left its limping horses, abandoned their lances and pennants and fled with the rest, their King leading them back through the thinning woodland to the castle keep and barricaded the doors. Their broken siege machines burned in the early evening and ravens watched the battlefield, biding their time.

Ke1 Bb4+

A Cleric approached. "My Lord, the men are tired and the enemy is beaten, let them rest."

The Lord nodded slowly. "I only need one of my machines," he said. "Find a Knight and go with them."

Before the castle walls the Cleric gave the trapped King his Lord's message. "If you surrender now you will be shown mercy!"

Kd1 Bb3+

Far above the shutters opened and grey faces stared down in silent defiance.

The Knight paraded his horse before the battlements and made threats, cast aspersions on his enemy's honour and ordered the siege machine to advance.

Kc1 Ne2+

An arrow loosed by an unseen hand glanced from the Knight's helm.

Kb1 Nc3+

"Then you will die here!" he shouted and lifted his sword for the advance.

The machine pounded the walls, splintered the doors, flung burning barrels of tar at the arrow slits. Screams drifted out into the evening.

Kc1 Rc2#

Hours later the Knight and the Cleric brought their enemy's standard to their Lord's tent.

"The defeat?" the Lord asked, his gruff voice at odds with his tender years.

"Total, my Lord," the Knight replied.

Only then did the Lord allow himself to smile and unfold a new map to plan fresh bloodshed.

The Knight grabbed his arm. "It's not a game lad. My men must rest."

The Knight met his Lord's eye and saw madness. He knew then that his master would never let the bloodshed stop.

It would never stop.

[The chess moves are from the endgame of "The Game of the Century" played between Donald Byrne and a 13-year old Bobby Fischer in the Rosenwald Memorial Tournament in New York City on October 17, 1956.]

At the tail in retreat, this is dangerous. One must not wish to undertake anything. A halted retreat is nerve-wracking and dangerous. Voluntary retreat brings good fortune to the superior man and downfall to the inferior man.

The Power of the Great

34. *Ta Chuang*

Miriam was organising her photographs, separating out the pictures of her parents during the war that had become mixed in with the other family snaps.

In the garden, George was zooming up and down the lawn with his toy aeroplane held high in pudgy fingers.

In one shot, her mum and dad stood in the garden, sepia toned and smiling amongst the endless rows of vegetables, the goats and their chickens surrounding them. In the background the old air raid shelter could just be seen behind the stand of runner beans.

George was swinging on the washing line, his plane forgotten in the grass.

In another, her father is at attention in his home guard uniform with the goat, the regimental mascot.

George was down on his knees inspecting a snail and poking at its shell with a stick.

One more of her mother, on her hands and knees stoking the fire in the living room, her apron streaked with black.

George was eating grass, green stems vanishing into his happy smiling mouth.

In this one, her father is at the door of the air raid shelter wrapped up warm against the cold and the goat, on the end of its rope, stands by his side.

George was knocking his head against the fence, tangling himself amongst the honeysuckle blooms. He fell, burst into tears and ran for the kitchen door.

Miriam was stroking her son's head, taking the twigs from his hair and wiping the grass stains from his mouth.

George was staring at her with his slotted, yellow eyes.

The last one, her parents, standing close together in the garden. Mother pregnant with her worried hands across her belly. Her father holding the goat.

The three of them before she came. Her parents and her brother.

A goat butts against a hedge and gets its horns entangled. The hedge opens; there is no entanglement. Loses the goat with ease. A goat butts against a hedge. It cannot go backward, it cannot go forward. Nothing serves to further.

Progress

35. Chin

Christmas morning. Under the covers Bobby was wound up tight, his fingers shaking in anticipation. He'd been as good as he could be considering he had a sister. He hadn't peeked through the banisters when he heard Santa shuffling about downstairs. He had cleaned his teeth and put himself to bed and lain in the glow of the closet light and wondered how long it would take for his chest to explode with excitement.

In the next room he could hear his father snoring, his mother turning over and muttering. His sister Jess was, as always, very quiet.

In his imagination he raced sports cars along their plastic tracks, flew spaceships across a glitter-covered blanket of stars all the while wearing a cowboy hat and toting six-shooter cap guns.

Comic books lay broken-backed on the carpet and were cold beneath his feet when he slid out of bed, the stairs sighing as he crept downwards, the living room a dark space full of unlit tree.

Then there were more footsteps and there was his

father, musty dressing gown and carpet slippers, yawning and fumbling for the light switch. Upstairs the bedsprings groaned as his mother rolled into the warm hollow he'd left behind.

"Hello, my little prince," Dad said.

They sat together and counted out the presents, made a pile for each of them, small things for Mum and Dad, big things for him.

"Do you only get small toys?" Bobby asked and yawned.

Dad smiled. "I have you," he said.

Bobby sat on the floor, his head sinking to his chest with a sigh. "It's all been a bit much for you, hasn't it?" Dad said and took the big key from the mantelpiece, slotted it into Bobby's back and gave a couple of sharp turns.

Bobby opened his eyes, smiled and leapt behind the tree to grab his present for his sister.

"Can I give it to her? Can I?" he asked.

"She'll be down with Mum," Dad said. "You know you're not allowed to wind your sister up."

"Aww, Dad!" Bobby whined. He unwrapped a box of wooden horses his mother had bought him and played with Dad until breakfast.

After lunch they sat and watched television, Dad with his big key and the rest of them ticking away happily, smiling.

Progress. The powerful prince is honoured with horses in large numbers. The sun rises over the earth: the image of Progress. Thus the superior man himself brightens his bright virtue. All are in accord. Remorse disappears.

Darkening of the Light

36. Ming I

Old man Roberts propped himself up on his barstool. One gnarled hand reached for another pretzel while the other brushed salt from his overalls.

"I was there in '65," he said. The other guys from the electric company, especially the younger ones, took note. Kenny Roberts rarely spoke and reminisced even less.

"I was in Brooklyn trying to get the power back online. That's when I met him."

Kenny took a swig of his beer.

"I didn't know what he was then," he continued. "Just a guy on the street in a black coat. Just a guy."

"After that was '71. I got called to the old Waterside plant on 40th and 1st after it exploded: Manhattan, the Bronx, Queens, all out. He was there too with his grey look and his coat wrapped 'round him like a bat, he looked at me like he recognized me, smiled, then just kinda shrugged like he was sorry for something."

"Then there was '77. Lightning took out Buchanan South. He was there drinking coffee on the corner watching the storm. I remember seeing him pointing at the sky, his coat flapping in the wind as another strike took out the transmission lines and, well you know the rest. That was a long three days."

The others nodded. The New York blackout was a legend by itself.

"Since then I've caught glimpses, under bridges or near old sub-stations, like he was there to kill the power and push the city back into the dark."

The old man took another swig.

"Then in '03 the whole Eastern seaboard went black. I wasn't out that night but went down anyway to help out. Halfway there I saw the guy. He was staring at all those stars you never see in New York."

"I walked over to him to say something, ask him why I'd always see him around when the power went out, like maybe I thought he had something to do with it."

"He didn't answer, just stood there, pointing up and moving his finger across the sky. So I grabbed him by the shoulder, got a good handful and then there was this flash, like the '77 lightning, and all I'm holding is his coat and there's this burning smell like hair and ozone and he's gone. Honest to God, just gone."

"So I'm looking up at where he was pointing and I see this one bright star just sort of going dim as I look at it. The news said it was one of them supernovas, but you couldn't have seen it with the naked eye if the lights had been on."

[On August 14th 2003 New York City was plunged into darkness after a 3,500 MW power surge caused by high demand for air-conditioning on such a hot day. That evening the Katzman Automated Imaging Telescope in San Jose, California detected the 2003hf supernova. The sky that night was perfectly clear.]

Darkening of the light during flight. He lowers his wings. But he has somewhere to go. Not light but darkness.

The Family (The Clan)

37. *Chia Jên*

The door to the hovel was thrown open and shuddered as it hit the wall. Out of the snow a great figure wrapped in animal hides appeared, stamped his feet, closed the door and nodded to the old woman at the fireside.

"Witch," he said, not an accusation but a greeting.

"Laird," she replied and pushed another log into the flames. She didn't get up. In her eyes they were equals.

Her two sisters watched from the shadows, one through the eyes of a crow hidden in the rafters, one as a toad who hid amongst her sister's aprons.

"The McDougals approach," the Laird said as he sat down.

The old woman gave the hulking man a cup of hot broth.

"A day away, maybe less when I left. I need your advice," he said. "And your help."

A low muttering came from the rafters.

"How can we live through this? They have more men and are better fed, our pride is no match for solid muscle."

"Survival, is that all?" the old woman asked.

"Aye, it is. That and no more," the Chieftain replied,

letting the broth warm the bones of his hands. "I'd spare my clan the fight if I can. They've wept enough."

The witch let her eye wander out over the fields, over the deep snow to the huddle of stone this man called home. She saw steel and running men and was glad she could not hear.

"Spare us this pain," the Laird said.

"I will do what I can," she said. Their eyes met in the firelight, hers full of steely resolve, his filled with the burden of his name.

The door slammed shut and the crow hopped down onto the table to peck at the dregs of broth.

"It's too late for the others," the crow said. The witch nodded, she could see the blood on the snow.

"Spare him the pain," the witch said. "That's what he wanted."

The toad, warm in the layers of hessian, kept her own council.

"He'll have to make it down the mountain, ride back across the valley," the crow mused.

"But if he fell and lost a shoe…" said the toad at last.

"And the cold had taken his horse…" added the crow.

"And the storm became worse…" they all said together and the words took root in the fire, breath from each of them leaping up the stone and mud and out into the sky.

"And then he'd be too late to see," the witch said to herself. "And that is the only pain we can take away from the world of men."

Wind comes forth from fire: The image of the Family. Thus the superior man has substance in his words and duration in his way of life. She is the treasure of the house. As a king he approaches his family. Fear not.

Opposition

38. K'uei

Halfway along Roupell Street the sound of the steam hammers on the new railway line was unbearable.

The crowds amongst the street stalls covered their ears and I wrapped my scarf around my head to blot out the infernal noise. A four-wheeled cart, pulled by great, filthy oxen, shuddered and collapsed as it was kicked to splinters by vast hooves.

Then, by God's mercy, the engines fell silent. I unwound my scarf and, stepping around the cart's broken wheels, made my way to the side door of the Kings Arms and saw Mister Prentice, much the worse for drink, holding onto the wall in the company of a woman.

The woman slid a coin into her purse and winked at me, leaving Mister Prentice to fasten his trews in full view of the street. I stood close to, with my back to Mister Prentice's fumblings to shield him from prying eyes.

His hand clasped my shoulder.

"Good lad. A good lad you are," he belched.

"I am gladdened by your appraisal, Sir," I replied as I helped him to stand a little straighter.

"And are you still bending your knee at the altar of the banking ledger?" he asked.

Mister Prentice had left me at my work more than two hours previously to run an errand.

"As you say, Sir," I replied carefully.

Workmen were pulling pieces of cart from the cobbles and a drover had unharnessed the oxen and was leading the white-eyed beasts away by their noses.

"You don't think much of me, do you boy?" Mister Prentice demanded.

He was, of course, a far more senior man at the bank than I and was much feared for his ruddy-faced shouting and fiercely critical eye.

"Well, answer me if you can!"

"We are each ourselves and no more, Sir," I replied, not daring to voice even the first glimmering of an opinion.

"Well then," Mister Prentice said. "We'll just keep this between us, shall we?"

"I cannot currently imagine a situation where revealing the details of this incident would be appropriate, Sir," I said.

"Yes, well, get to it then. I'm sure you've been away from your ledger long enough."

I tested my position. "Do you have a shilling I can borrow, Sir, only my trousers are filthy and I can hardly go back to the bank smelling of…" and before I could finish the coin was in my hand.

The alley girl approached me as Mister Prentice left in a hansom.

"There you go girl," I said, giving her the shilling.

"Do you want me to send another message if any of the other fine gentlemen from the bank come and, you know?"

I hushed her to silence.

"Now," she said, "what do you suppose I should do with a gent who just gave me a shilling?"

When you see evil people, guard yourself against mistakes. One meets his lord in a narrow street. One sees the wagon dragged back, the oxen halt. Isolated through opposition, one meets a like-minded man with whom one can associate in good faith, despite the danger.

Obstruction

39. Chien

The garbage man sings opera. You can hear him over the hydraulics and the clattering of the bins.

"*Scartati!*" he sings, his mouth wide to give the hurricane in his lungs somewhere to go.

"*Scartati! Abbandonato! Indesiderato!*"

(Discarded! Abandoned! Unwanted!)

I open my bedroom window and close my eyes to hear.

"*Questo è quello che hai fatto!*"

(That's what you did!)

"*E ora non mi lascia in casa!*"

(And now you won't let me in the house!)

Then I realize.

He's not singing opera. It's the blues.

The king's servant is beset by obstruction upon obstruction, but it is not his own fault. Going leads to obstructions; hence he comes back. In the midst of the greatest obstructions, friends come.

Deliverance

40. *Hsieh*

"It was like being at war, I suppose," the Professor said.

He relaxed deeper into his red leather armchair and sipped his brandy in the candlelight.

His wife raised an eyebrow and stuck the poker into the remains of the fire before retrieving her cup of tea.

"Not battles. Not soldiers in the trenches. That's not what I mean." He stared at the last flames in the hearth.

"It was a race to be first," he began again. "The speed of sound, the moon landing, you know the kind of thing."

"The atom bomb?" she asked.

"Precisely," he replied.

She knew not to pry any further. He'd always known how to keep a secret. All she knew was that deep in the Atacama Desert was a machine and it had kept her husband from her.

"It was difficult," he said at last.

"The work?"

"Missing you."

She reached across the gap between them and gently squeezed his hand.

"Not being able to call, not even being allowed to write a letter, that was the hardest thing to stomach."

His wife closed her eyes and let him talk. Four years of pent up thoughts rolled across the carpet.

"I wondered if you'd changed," he said. "I had your photograph by my bed and wondered if you'd cut your hair or decided on a new favourite dress. It became hard to remember you."

She put her hand up to her curls and ran her hand through the auburn and the grey.

"It's strange how some things are hard to recollect, the little details," he said. "But that place we used to go to for tea on the square, the rickety tables and the homemade cakes, as clear as day. I used to dream about it."

"And the sofa by the fire," she said.

In the deep orange glow her husband smiled.

"Yes, all those crumbs under the cushions," he said. "What were they? Coconut? Banana bread?"

"Almonds," she said.

"Oh yes. Crushed almonds, that wonderful smell."

Her husband had come home early. Homesickness he'd said, but she suspected.

"I love you, Julie," he said.

She turned to face him.

"Judith," she said.

If there is no longer anything where one has to go, return brings good fortune. If there is still something where one has to go, hastening brings good fortune.

Decrease

41. *Sun*

Harry stood in the queue while his sisters gossiped ahead of him and whispered slanders into each other's ears.

Maureen and Dorothy were older, tidy women. He had come along just after the war and they had treated him as a doll, a toy and an inconvenience, but not necessarily in that order.

These days he helped them tighten cupboard doors, unblock drains and anything else they wouldn't lower themselves to do.

He'd only been allowed to come because he needed flex and a fuse for a broken lamp, so he had shuffled around the store and listened as they tutted about the prices, the size of the portions and which of the additives would give them both cancer.

At the till they discussed last night's bingo, who had won what, who had sat with whom, who had said what and what, if anything, it all meant.

The woman at the till was scanning and packing their shopping, slipping each item into the hessian bags his sisters had bought to save the planet from American cars and homosexuals.

Harry liked the checkout lady, her name badge said Sarah and Harry was always polite and always said thank you when she gave him his receipt. He'd seen her on the bus once or twice, getting off two stops before him on that nice street that used to have all those trees.

People like Sarah were invisible to Maureen and Dorothy, just like the postman, the bus conductor, and anybody else who performed essential, but in their eyes menial, jobs. Their gaze just slid off them until they focused on something worthy of their attention, such as finding fault with Harry.

His sisters talked and only paused to peer over their glasses at the credit card machine and hesitantly type out the PIN number in mortal fear of this identity theft business they'd read so much about in the papers. They placed their bags in their trolley and wandered off towards the car park still gossiping.

Sarah smiled at Harry as he bagged his flex and fuses, raised an eyebrow at his photography magazine and gently pushed his meals for one through the scanner.

"I'm doing a course at the college," she said.

"Oh, er, really?" said Harry. "What kind of course?"

Sarah helped him pack the rest of his bags. "Photography," she said. "I'm only a beginner, but I really enjoy it."

"Yes, so do I. I'm trying to do black and whites at the minute. It's a lot harder than it looks."

"I'll say," Sarah replied. "We had a demonstration last month but I couldn't make mine look the same. Why don't you come along? It's Thursday nights."

Sarah took the receipt from the till, handed him his change.

"Hope to see you there," she said.

Harry thought about what his sisters would say, their brother cavorting with a shop girl. It would give the rest of the bingo lot something to talk about, that's for sure.

Then, on his way back to the car, he remembered that his sisters would never allow themselves to see or acknowledge a supermarket employee, even if she was right in front of them, or on Harry's arm.

So that was all right then.

When three people journey together, their number decreases by one. When one man journeys alone, he finds a companion.

Increase

42. *Yì*

"I like stuttering." she wrote in her notebook.

She showed it to the therapist, who frowned.

"How can I cure your stutter if you like it?" he asked.

Amy wrote, "Stuttering slows me down. I have to think about it and it stops me saying anything stupid, or nasty."

The therapist read this.

"Proverbs 13:3," he said. "He who guards his lips guards his life, but he who speaks rashly will come to ruin."

Amy shrugged. "Mum told me to 'Say something nice or say nothing.' Dad mostly said 'Shut up with your ner-ner-ner and your ger-ger-ger! I'm sick of it.'" she wrote.

"But you don't live at home anymore," the therapist said.

Amy swallowed and licked her lips. "No. I d-don't," she said.

"And how long have you had a stutter?" he asked.

"I taught myself. When I was ten nearly eleven." she wrote.

"You taught yourself?" the therapist was stunned. "You made yourself stutter?"

This time the handwriting leapt across the page. "Yes, because of my parents. I couldn't talk back. It helped me. Stopped any more shouting and being shut in my room and the hitting."

She looked her therapist right in the eye and concentrated.

"B-bastards."

Wind and thunder: the image of Increase. Thus the superior man: If he sees good, he imitates it; if he has faults, he rids himself of them.

Break-through (Resoluteness)

43. *Kuai*

"Oh, God, now what?"

The letter had arrived innocuously with the rest but the dreaded city council crest was a red and angry boil amongst the bills.

"Dear Mr Prough," it began. This was an ominous start. Polite letters from the council always meant trouble, especially the ones that ended with 'compulsory redundancy' and 'pension shortfall'.

"It has come to our attention… rules and regulations… paragraph 6b of the agreement… flagrant disregard," he muttered.

All this about a bloody allotment.

He'd taken over the plot after the lawyers explained to him that the council was acting lawfully and could retire him any time it wished.

The ground had been high with grass and brambles but he had cleared it and taken all the skin off his knuckles and ruined several stout pairs of trousers in the process.

One vicious rose had dragged its thorns across his legs and he'd gone for tetanus shots just to be sure.

He'd dug through the rain, picked the flints out of the sod and cursed and swore as the other growers laughed at him and said he'd never grow anything, not in that soil.

He'd tried carrots but they rotted in the ground.

Someone said "I told you so" and he'd let them know exactly what he thought about that. It took some time and a very loud voice.

Next he tried peas and a few potatoes. The birds ate the peas. The potatoes grew around the flints and came out of the ground like medieval weapons, a cross between a cat o' nine tails and a mace. He threw them away.

He watched the relentless rain and thought about growing rice, but didn't.

So instead he decided to grow weeds.

The first letter from the council had arrived two days later.

"Fruit, vegetables and ornamental plants only" it had reminded him. Paragraph 6b again.

He wrote back explaining his predicament. That only produced another letter, then another.

But Mr Prough kept going. He built a frame for his Russian vine, kept Japanese Knotweed in a pot, cultivated Bindweed and Milk Thistle and much else besides until he had two thousand square feet of poisonous, glorious, unstoppable colour.

He entered a national completion for alternative gardening and won second prize.

Then he went to the papers.

The following morning there was a letter from the council.

"Sir, we apologise for the accidental spillage of a small amount of a controlled herbicide at the site on Garbett Road," it began. When he went to see, the leaves were already blackening.

But that was the thing with weeds, Mr Prough thought as the breeze carried his seeds over his neighbour's tomatoes and out towards the council's perfect lawns, there was always next year.

It must be announced truthfully. Danger. It is necessary to notify one's own city. He is bespattered, and people murmur against him. There is no skin on his thighs, and walking comes hard. In dealing with weeds, firm resolution is necessary.

Coming to Meet

44. *Kou*

Rusted at the bottom, bird-spattered white at the top, the funfair gates hang open, stuck that way after the rides burned down.

A boy and a girl, hair in the wind and sun-bleached shirts.

That's what we were.

And you ran faster and I chased after through the place that was: candies and prizes of fish, apple caramel on waxed and painted boards. Nothing to see now.

But, on a summer's day, if the hammer hadn't been so brightly striped it wouldn't have caught your eye and the older boys wouldn't have cheered you on. It was just a game for us to play.

The bell ringing in my head.

In my hands the hammer's head was taller, broader than my shoulders. I swung and missed then swung again and hit and there was only silence.

"Not even as strong as a girl!" they laughed.

You looked at me then, with something in your eyes like disappointment.

Just a boy, skinny arms and red eyes, shouting back, fists flailing.

That was what I was, the day you burned me down.

The maiden is powerful. One should not marry such a maiden. If one lets it take its course, one experiences misfortune. Even a lean pig has it in him to rage around.

Gathering Together (Massing)

45. *Ts'ui*

He struggled on with four across over a cup of tea, the 'z' making him frown as outside the windows the trees bent and cracked as the autumn leaves spiralled and whipped themselves against the window.

"Memory loss baffles hazel miser, ten letters," he said to himself.

While buttering his toast, he tried to remember the patron saint of salt miners, another word that wasn't in the dictionary and should have been on the tip of his tongue.

As he peered into the cupboard for jam the Latin word for 'duck' interrupted him. He struggled with the lid. Then he wrote it down.

The broken kettle boiled and boiled, fogging his glasses. He spilled the sugar, the teaspoon shaking. He wiped his lenses and grappled with his hesitant mis-spellings of the answer for eighteen down.

The deconstruction of twenty-five across was a subtle combination of initials, abbreviations and double mean-ings that made him smile but he double-checked it just to be sure.

The crossword finished he took a card-backed envelope and slid it inside on the third attempt, off to be printed in tomorrow's paper. His fingers trembled as he licked the stamp.

His pseudonym on the bottom right of the puzzle would send shivers through the Friday commuters. Sometimes he travelled with them, read a book and watched their furrowed brows, the endless crossing out, the beatific look of completion, the conqueror's moment.

Keep your weapons sharp and you'll be ready for anything, he thought, and there is no greater weapon than the mind.

Beyond his window, fog rolled over the fields and, branch by branch, obscured the autumn trees.

Thus the superior man renews his weapons in order to meet the unforeseen. If there are some who are not yet sincerely in the work, sublime and enduring perseverance is needed. Then remorse disappears.

Pushing Upward

46. *Shêng*

Granddad had taken me for a walk along the narrow pavements to the seafront to watch the gulls and eat chips. Granddad took a couple for himself then gave me the paper cone as we sat on a bench and talked, my blue shoes just brushing the ground and his greatcoat wrapped around both our shoulders.

He saw a poppy seller and gave me a bent penny to put in the tin. He pinned the flower on my dungarees and took my hand and tipped his hat at the memorial as we passed.

"Why did you give me a bent penny?" I asked.

"So God knows it was yours and you've been a good boy," Granddad said.

He took another from his pocket, flat and shiny, and pressed it between his fingers.

"Hold out your hand," he said.

The penny was old and brown and bent.

"Magic!" I shouted. "Show me again."

"I haven't got any more."

We walked back through the park, my pockets soon full of shiny conkers.

Near our street a tree had fallen during the storm, its limbs tangled and broken on the spiky railings.

"Shall I plant a tree?" I asked.

"Plant everything you've got lad, then we'll know at least one will come through," Granddad said.

So we dug a trench in the cold mud with sticks, pushed the conkers in with our fingers and threw dirt over them when we were done.

Granddad buried the bent penny with them.

"So when it's spring they'll remember you," he said.

Thus the superior man of devoted character heaps up small things in order to achieve something high and great.

Oppression (Exhaustion)

47. *K'un*

"I love you," he said.

"I wish you'd say it like you meant it," she said.

"Cut!" Richard shouted. "Look Tommy darling, I know Debbie is a miserable old bag with fat-ankles, but we don't have to let the audience know that, do we? So, again."

Tom moved back to the taped yellow cross, stepped through an imaginary door and stood apologetically with a bunch of plastic flowers in his hand projecting heterosexual despair.

"I love you," he begged.

"I wish you'd say it like you meant it," Debbie spat back.

"How can you say that?" Tom sobbed. The flowers dropped to the floor.

"Better!" Richard clapped his hands together. "Now Debbie, we're going to need lashings of extra bitch for the next bit, and don't try and tell me you don't have it in you, you're not fooling anyone."

Debbie threw her script at the director and burst into tears.

During the emergency break for Manhattans and hugs Tom sat backstage under the bare branches of a plywood forest. A painted lake complete with lilies and plastic ducks was propped against the wall ready for the melodramatic bit in the second act.

Tom flipped though his lines to Act Two, Scene Two.

"What can I do?" he proclaimed. "Every movement brings remorse, every message compounds rejection. I am undone!"

Richard popped his head around the corner and came to hold Tom's hand. "Oh, keep going darling, it all sounds rather good. Anyway, Debbie's drunk enough not to care any more so shall we get on? Love you!"

Tom rolled up his script and trudged back on stage.

"I love you," he said.

"No, no, no, darling!" Richard shouted. "With *feeling*!"

When one has something to say, it is not believed. There is no water in the lake: One sits oppressed under a bare tree. Misfortune. He moves uncertainly and says, "Movement brings remorse."

The Well

48. *Ching*

Saleh's wife poked at the last loaf on the shelf. The familiar sound of her complaining carried out onto the street and was whipped away by the dusty breeze.

"Six months digging a well," she continued. "You'd have thought that would be the end of it, but no! Always there is something more to do!"

Two women, her only customers, huddled by the bare shelves, eyed the last loaf and plotted their escape.

From the back of the shop the insistent sound of hammers and spanners ground on unabated.

"He says it'll be fixed tomorrow, always tomorrow! So I have to listen to the noise and apologise for my empty shop. No wonder the bakery of Ahmed is so busy, he doesn't have a retired engineer in his shop, just bread."

"And now the rope has snapped and the bucket has fallen in and there is sand in the bread and he just stands there, scratching his head!"

One of the women in the queue nodded and made for the door, fine sand billowing on the shop floor as it shut behind her.

All the way down the road the woman could hear the endless complaints of Saleh's wife stinging her ears.

She joined the queue for Ahmed's shop, women talking softly together as the smell of freshly baked bread crept amongst them.

Another woman came to join them, a fresh loaf beneath her arm wrapped in cloth.

"This bread is terrible," she said quietly.

"I know, Saleh's bread was soft and sweet, his loaves were bigger too," said another.

"But his wife! Oh, what a tongue she has, and her voice!"

"Yes, like vinegar!"

"It sours the bread on the shelves," someone said and laughed.

Back at Saleh's shop, Saleh's wife was standing at her husband's bedside and seeing to his bandages.

"Do they suspect?" he asked her.

"No, husband, they do not. Every day they hear you working. Your honour is intact."

"You are a wonder," he said.

Below them in the bakery the hammers and spanners twirled on strings in the desert breeze and clanged against the empty pans and made a busy noise.

The Well. The town may be changed, but the well cannot be changed. It neither decreases nor increases. They come and go and draw from the well. If the jug breaks, it brings misfortune. The well is cleaned, but no one drinks from it. This is my heart's sorrow, for one might draw from it.

Revolution (Molting)

49. *Ko*

"God save the King!" they all shouted, raising their tankards and taking a draught.

"And a Happy New Year!" shouted a voice from the back.

There was a collective groan in the tavern.

"Who is that?" asked a young squire.

The merchant Cartwright slapped the squire on the back. "That, young Sir, is a Fool! Old Man Smith has yet to embrace the modern age!"

"It's not right!" the old man protested. "One day it is Wednesday the second of September the next it is Thursday the fourteenth September. Then they tell us New Year's Day is January the First, not today, the twenty-fifth of March! It's a Papist plot that has our good King under its thrall!"

"Do you say our good King George is a fool, Sir?" Cartwright challenged. "These are God's days, not the days of Caesar! And did not those of you in the Crown's employ receive payment for the Days of God?"

There was a rousing cheer at the bar.

"And who are the only men who stick to the old ways?

The bankers of the Lords and the astrologers of the gullible!"

Another cheer.

"And do we not think that the King is mightier than these money men and soothsayers. What say you?"

A final cheer erupted with many shouts of "The King!"

"So, there you have it," Cartwright concluded. "Our King can decide the date for himself and damn and blast what old men say! You will move with the times or you will die!"

"But that is where you are wrong!" the old man shouted, rising from his bench in triumph. "I have moved with the times and now I possess a way to use the days each of you gave up! Eleven days from every man in England, nay, every man, woman and child! I will outlive you all!" And with that old man Smith slammed his tankard down, leapt across the table and rushed out into the night.

The young squire finished his drink and took another from a wench's tray.

"How old is that old man?" he asked the merchant.

"Seventy, if he's a day," Cartwright said. "Why say you?"

"No reason, Sir," the young squire said. "But my God, can he run!"

[On Wednesday the second of September 1752 the Julian calendar changed into the Gregorian. The eleven "Days of God" that ended on the fourteenth of September were never seen again.}

Thus the superior man sets the calendar in order and makes the seasons clear. When talk of revolution has gone the rounds three times, one may commit himself, and men will believe him.

The Cauldron

50. Ting

The storm had passed. From the rafters of the witch's cottage the crow, her sister, fluttered down on black wings to settle on her shoulder. From the apron pocket there was silence as the toad slept on.

"We must go now," said the crow.

The witch looked into the fire, withdrew her mind from the forest and the mountainside, put her hand on the toad's back and the crow's wing, and stepped into the flames.

They travelled as smoke against the wind, through the valley to the field at the edge of the trees where the stone houses stood beside the river.

The smoke drew itself to a hearth and the witch stepped out.

Bodies had been placed in a pyre and long since turned to ash. Survivors worked to sharpen their swords and cook whatever food remained in a great iron pot with a broken foot.

The Laird stood before them.

"Survival. That's what I asked for," he said.

The witch cast her eyes over the village. "And the McDougals?" she asked.

"All dead. We met them with steel and cunning. The storm was thick and the snow blinded them. We know this land well.

We took the McDougals into the forest, waited for them to lose themselves then left them for the wolves. It was a slaughter."

"Aye, I can see that. What will you do now Laird?"

"Rebuild, hunt, plant crops. Live."

The witch nodded. Overhead the crow flew in long circles over the village.

The Laird took a bowl, filled it and offered it to the witch. They sat in silence, ate and watched the flames.

Between the trees there was only silence.

"Bless this place," she said.

"Thank you, witch," the Laird replied.

Soon the sisters were smoke again, travelling with the wind along the valley.

In their cottage the crow sat on the table and straightened her feathers.

"What the Laird said…" the crow began.

"I know," the witch replied.

"The wolves in these forests moved on before the storm," the crow continued.

"Aye, and yet the McDougals are dead. That's what worries me sister."

The toad appeared from her warm pocket.

"There is something…" she croaked.

The witch's eyes were drawn away from the flames in the hearth to the great, black shadows of the crow's feathers on the wall, and in her mind she could feel the furnace breath and hear the sound of leathery wings.

On the crest of the mountainside a warrior, a woman, sat astride her horse. With a kick the dragonslayer urged her mount down into the valley and emptied the bag of great, yellow teeth behind her as she went.

Fire over wood: The image of the Cauldron. Thus the superior man consolidates his fate by making his position correct. The legs of the cauldron are broken. Misfortune.

The Arousing (Shock, Thunder)

51. Chên

Me an Beth'd been arguin, just driving along behind the old Packard place. She was flappin her gums about some junk she'd seen on TV and I was yakking at her bout some other stuff I'd read in a magazine. We were having a great time giving each other shit and we were goin at it pretty good.

Beth'd heard about make-up sex, so she argued with me every chance she got.

Then Old Man Packard comes out of his gate in his John Deere, not even looking, and everythin went real slow. I could see the tractor tyres coming up, felt my boot on the brake, heard Beth begin to shout, then the hula girl on my dash just kinda floated up into the air as the car behind slammed right into the back of us and I hit the tractor side on.

Thump. Thump.

I woke up in Nine Hills. The doctors and nurses came and went, told me to wait and rest a while and I tried to make myself comfortable, surrounded by all the blinking and the beeping.

There were painkillers and sleeping pills day after day

but every time I asked a question the staff just smiled that sad little smile my vet had when we put the dog down.

Then, like a week later, some guy comes and shakes me awake and tells me to grab my stuff. So I peel myself off the waiting room chair and go up into the ward and through all them bendy plastic doors until I'm standing next to Beth's bed.

She looks banged up pretty good, black and blue and one arm in plaster. She's sleepin, they tell me, and she has been since she came in, but she's okay and I got nothin to worry about.

I pull a chair over and sit my sorry ass down. One bruise, two scrapes and seatbelt burn is all I have to show for sideswipin my wife into a tractor.

When she wakes up there's going to be hell to pay and the thought of arguin with Beth again makes me feel damn good.

I put my head on her chest and listen to her breathe and below the gentle sighs of life I can hear her heart beating.

Thump. Thump.

Thunder repeated: the image of Shock. Thus in fear and trembling the superior man sets his life in order and examines himself. You lose your treasures and must climb the nine hills. Do not go in pursuit of them. After seven days you will get them back.

Keeping Still, Mountain

52. Kên

After the accident she came home rebuilt.

At breakfast, the platinum beneath her skin glows, pulsing with electricity, curiously alive.

I take some toast, spread butter. I see that there are no eggs in the pan.

She smiles, a mechanical lighthouse across the blue ocean of tablecloth. Her head turns smoothly towards the window, her warmth coming only from the sun.

I open my newspaper setting the pages full sail, seeking guidance in the new star of her unreadable face, in the night of her eyes.

Tonight I know I will not dream of her, only of the sea.

Keeping his back still so that he no longer feels his body. He goes into his courtyard and does not see his people. No blame. His heart is not glad. The heart suffocates. The words have order.

Development (Gradual Progress)

53. *Chien*

Genarro's latest sculpture stood, arms outstretched, the face touched with a grace he knew he'd never make again. It was as if the supple wood had known what it would become, forming under his planes and chisels until she had sprung from the tree he'd chosen, a dryad from the unforgiving mountainside.

She was to be delivered to Raffaello's boutique, to stand in the window dressed in the latest fashions, a commission from the old man who had wandered around his exhibition and had stood spellbound, his face glowing.

Genarro caressed every curve, putting off the inevitable. She was so beautiful it made him sick at the thought of putting her in a crate and sending her away.

He did not go to the grand unveiling, a shop window was not the place for her.

The next day Raffaello called him, begged him to come.

There were crowds in the street jostling for position; men with their hats in their hands, wearing their best suits, gazed silently. Some had flowers.

"It's a disaster!" Rafaello moaned. He had collapsed in an armchair and was mopping his brow. "Everyone comes, but they only come for her! No one comes in. Nobody buys! Just for her!"

Within the display she was poised, floating in space in a simple dress with feathers in her hair; the clouds beneath were full of birds as her outstretched hands caressed the wings of geese. Raffaello had made her weightless, ethereal, impossibly more beautiful than before.

Raffaello pleaded with him. "Make me another that my clothes will make beautiful! Make me another and make her plain!"

As Genarro hurried home the pavement was filling up with flowers, tearful, yearning men and the burning stares of jealous wives who stood, stony-faced, like the crags of the mountainside.

On the mountain, a tree: The image of Development. The wild goose gradually draws near the cloud heights. Its feathers can be used for the sacred dance.

The Marrying Maiden

54. *Kuei Mei*

At dawn, with the full moon still in the sky and the locked door of the church before him, Father Edward knelt on the path and brushed his fingers over the dew in the unkempt grass.

Here, a footprint, and there, another; stalks flattened by last night's hooves and revelries.

There, a cobweb, fallen from her dress to lie amongst the green, glittering and delicate, like the shape of her arms as she moved to the music he could not hear.

He'd stood in the street and watched over the wall, their indistinct shapes encircling the graveyard yew, their clothes no more than rags, their bodies free and joyful, intertwined in their celebration.

Beyond, the church squats in its stony disapproval. The music there is not for dancing, the source of joy is distant and intangible; that face is turned away and wreathed in blue and white. Her eyes are only for the child in her arms, he the Saviour and she his Mother.

He longed to jump the wall, strip off his vestments and join them, but he'd not dared. She was like the mist and as skittish as a fawn. If he'd moved he would have startled her, he thought, and she would have faded away and left only his desire behind her.

Now, in the dawn of All Soul's Day, he prepares himself for the service of another year, but in his heart there is only the dance.

The marrying maiden draws out the allotted time. A late marriage comes in due course. The embroidered garments of the princess were not as gorgeous as those of the serving maid. The moon that is nearly full brings good fortune. Thus the superior man understands the transitory in the light of the eternity of the end.

Abundance (Fullness)

55. *Fêng*

The moon had waxed to nothing. Professor Malcolm pressed his eye to the telescope and gently turned the reflector to a new constellation. Beside him his hand wrote automatically, his pencil carefully noting inclinations and declinations, time and date in neat columns as he settled down, took a sip of brandy and waited.

Retirement suited him. He did exactly what he had done every day at work, only in an armchair in his upstairs study with his slippers on.

Faded wedding photos and baby pictures sat forgotten and faded in a cardboard box, his awards and gold medals sat in another with a new packet of picture hooks and a hammer with the price tag still on it.

Through the eyepiece the Professor saw endless galaxies, the hidden lairs of black holes, the embers of supernovae all as familiar to him as the fingers of his hands. He smiled at the recollection of discovery, the thrill, the congratulations. It all seemed so far away.

He finished his brandy and wrapped himself in his

dressing gown, struggled with his slippers and made his way downstairs for dinner, his first in this house for as long as he could remember.

The dining room door swung open on a crowd, raised glasses and broad smiles welcoming their father back from decades staring at the night sky. Diamonds and cut glass glittered, silver cutlery sparkled in the candlelight. As he was led amongst them to his place at the head of the table he looked at each welcoming face and shook their hands.

These were his family, strangers who had loved him all the years he'd been away and, bathed in their light and warmth, he drank a glass of wine and began again, cataloguing one bright sun after another.

His house is in a state of abundance. He screens off his family. He peers through the gate and no longer perceives anyone. For three years he sees nothing. Misfortune.

The Wanderer

56. *Lu*

The hotel room burned. Their argument melted the carpet; her brimstone accusations sent their flames up the curtains and reduced the chairs to ash; his wedding ring, on a chain around his neck, molten in the furnace of his infidelity.

She'd tried to run, to fly down the bright corridors and breathe the cool air but his words pierced her, the arrows of his lies finding her heart and her head as she cowered in the bathroom, his ugliness reflected in every surface.

She slid to the floor and sobbed, pulling the taps as she went, the shower raining iced water on her face as he sat upon the smouldering bed, the sheets still cooling from the first fires of the night.

He was laughing, apologising, his words a sly conciliation. He knew that he was wrong, knew she was wrong for letting him free. This was their arrangement, to fly apart and then nest together when the need ignited them. We are Phoenixes, he said, burning for each other, setting the world alight.

But she'd seen her gift around his neck, seen its empty

place on his left hand and knew that there had been other feathers on these crisp, white sheets.

In the shower her shimmering flames extinguished, the water cooled her to the core until she knew she would fly once more but burn no more.

On the bed, a middle-aged man in his boxer shorts whispered his last, his broken arrows falling to the carpet as his tears failed to douse the flaming heart, the fire that was never there.

The wanderer's inn burns down, he loses the steadfastness of his young servant. The wanderer rests in a shelter. He shoots a pheasant, it drops with the first arrow. The bird's nest burns up. The wanderer laughs at first, then must needs lament and weep. Misfortune.

The Gentle (The Penetrating, Wind)

57. *Sun*

The caravan had pitched on the bare fields of an abandoned farm outside of town. Later the troupe paraded down the main street, their handbills flying on the evening wind as the ringmaster threw them from his bag.

"Roll up Dakota! Roll up for the Carnival of '34!" came the shout, and roll up they did to pay their two bits and see the show.

The grand spectacle was one small tent and a handful of sideshows. Under cover of darkness with fire breathers and jugglers making long shadows in the dirt, the townsfolk and the farmers of the ruined earth came to watch and were amazed.

The cotton candy machine sold out in half an hour. The fat lady, exhausted from so many stares, retreated to her bed. Men dressed as lions put their heads in the mouths of painted crocodiles and a fearsome pumpkin tamer showed the children how to catch and carve without being bitten.

Soon, with so few acts and such numbers of visitors, even the stagehands and set painters did their turn, dropping their batons and falling over each other until the visitors laughed and threw their hats into the air.

The ringmaster pushed on his last act, a small boy in a jacket three sizes too big.

The boy stood, twitching and shaking, his fingers clenched in his sleeves, mumbling his practiced words while the crowd called for him to speak up, speak up and show us magic.

The ringmaster saw the opportunity and waved for silence. He stalked to and fro before the crowd, goaded them with tales of great wizardry and the cost of real magic. The crowd threw coins and waited. The boy, still terrified and having forgotten all his tricks, began to cry.

The crowd saw the tears run down his face, leave streaks through his crude makeup and fall onto the barren land as a new, chill wind came howling from the south and blew the striped flags taut against the tent-poles. And then it rained.

The farmers whooped and hollered, the women hugged each other and the children hid inside the tent and underneath the wooden carts to watch their parents dancing, dancing, dancing at the end of dust.

[In 1933, a dust storm stripped the topsoil from the dry South Dakota farmlands then, beginning on May 9, 1934, a two-day storm took over 12 million pounds of topsoil from the Great Plains and blew clouds all the way to Chicago. In the winter of '34 – '35 red snow fell on New England.]

Winds following one upon the other: The image of the Gently Penetrating. Priests and magicians are used in great number. Good fortune. No blame.

The Joyous, Lake

58. Tui

He hung up his coat and shook the rain from his umbrella. He was telling a joke by the time he got to the bar.

"Good old Eddie," they all said and laughed along.

He had a flippant comment for everyone's troubles and grinned his happy grin at every put down, mistaking it for wit.

And when he left they all slapped him on the back and wished him well and said, "Good old Eddie," one more time.

Outside it was still raining, a lake falling from the sky and laughing down the gutters.

He went back for his forgotten umbrella, saw the shapes of their mouths as they talked quietly of sensible things, offered each other good advice and invited each other to dinner.

He was "That guy. Eddie." and he knew it from the laughter that didn't fall from their sensible mouths.

He bought a cup of tea and sat quietly in a corner, listened to them talk and waited for the rain to stop.

Thus the superior man joins with his friends for discussion and practice. Contented joyousness. Joyousness that is weighed is not at peace. After ridding himself of mistakes a man has joy.

Dispersion (Dissolution)

59. *Huan*

George had hidden in the dining room to drink his brandy and get a bit of peace and quiet from the kids and the grandkids.

He sat down groaning and puffing, kicked his slippers off and found a place for his glass. Under the endless wrapping paper he found Margaret's jigsaw, a present from their daughter, Susan. She'd taken a photo of her mum and dad, sitting quietly in the living room surrounded by books and cats, and sent it off to be made into a puzzle.

Margaret had loved it and spent a few happy hours finding all the edges while Susan did wonders with the Christmas dinner.

George started to put the pieces back in the box.

One showed the wooden house god he'd brought back from Africa, squat and heavy, its serene eyes staring. He held up the piece and saw how it slotted together with another, proper wood, not cardboard. George approved.

The books they'd collected were all there. Every leather spine, every orange and white, old-fashioned paperback they'd brought with them from London, all those happy hours spent rummaging the stalls under Waterloo bridge. George hadn't thought of that for years.

Here was their wedding photo, silver framed and full of smiles with a billow in Margaret's dress behind which Susan was already on the way.

Another piece held Tony, his baby picture up on the shelf, then Roger's tiny footprints in clay next to that.

He carefully undid the last few pieces and put them away, all except the last. He ran his thumb over the curves and hollows that held his wife's face. So many years, so many pieces to their own puzzle that fitted together just so, as if this life had been made for them.

He closed the lid, put the box on a shelf and stared out into the garden and finished his brandy.

So many pieces perfectly slotted together, George thought.

He slid his feet into his new slippers, shuffled across the carpet and opened the living room door.

Here are all the pieces, shelves full of memories and gifts, and on the floor, gathered around the fire are Susan and Tony and Roger and their wives and their children, all of them making space for each other, or held in each other's arms. Perfect.

Here comes Margaret with a plate of warm mince pies and everyone turns to look and smile at Grandma and Grandpa.

Not edge, but middle.

He dissolves his bond with his group. Dispersion leads in turn to accumulation. This is something that ordinary men do not think of.

Limitation

60. *Chieh*

I am not a poet, but there has to be another way, the Professor thinks. It seems unfair that I can only mark you out of ten. You are my daughter, and there is so much more to you than integers can ever measure.

He works and finds another number, plucks it from a strange equation and places it amongst the rest where it fits quite naturally, it seems to him.

The equation squirms on the board as he burrows into it with chalk, making it give up all its secrets and solutions.

This is subtlety, he thinks. This is elegance and grace within numbers. These are the numbers you deserve.

Diving into new expressions, he finds yet more to add to the ever-expanding row of ten. New symbols leap and insinuate themselves into the list until there is no space to add another, no more room for how much he wanted to tell her what a daughter means.

On the board the list begins at one then twists, moves through his weird dimensions, before it becomes two and then three.

Between eight and nine a contradiction lurks, two

numbers simultaneously the same yet different, one prime, the other not, a single integer. Impossible.

He could not stop, would not dare to stop. Once begun, the new sprang from him, imaginary and limitless without a care for consequence. He makes these numbers for her, speaks their names and sets them free.

He tries to call to tell her, but the dial on the telephone is impossible to read, its circle face bulging into strange geometries in the gaps between the numbers.

He wants so very much to call, but the line is dead and her number is no longer real.

Yes, he thinks, exactly right.

Thus the superior man creates number and measure, and examines the nature of virtue and correct conduct. He who knows no limitation will have cause to lament.

Inner Truth

61. *Chung Fu*

A video call is not the same as you, nor is text or telephone. An email will simply not suffice, nor any social media shared as you sway on the morning train.

A letter is more like you than that, as your handwriting flows and loops over the stain left by your coffee cup.

You do not write. You embrace the latest gadget, the newest thing that will, you think, project you to the four corners of the earth and let your loved ones see your shining essence, glowing and insubstantial, wafer-thin in LEDs.

Being intimately separated, divided by small, gentle energies, is not the same for me. You say that soon devices will allow us all to touch across the miles. But, I ask, how will it know when I simply need to hold your hand and share a smile without a word exchanged?

I rebel and smash my screen against this edge, its crack and tinkling silence will, I hope, elicit some response. I await a query from your chirping self that will say 'Where are you?' and with my silence your curiosity will rise until you must return to see if I am still alive, still breathing.

I want you to know that I am really here in flesh and faded corduroy and not some simple algorithm or clever app that automatically hits 'like'.

If there are secret designs, it is disquieting. He finds a comrade. Now he beats the drum, now he stops. Now he sobs, now he sings. He possesses truth, which links together.

Preponderance of the Small

62. *Hsiao Kuo*

On the long benches near the fire the Generals argued over the great game. It had been days since the last move and from this position any side could steal victory.

The King held his chin in his hand and listened as the reasons for the next move were explained.

Satisfied, he asked for a vote, a show of hands, proof that this was the best way to proceed. There was a majority and the Master of The Pigeons was summoned. Then, with no small ceremony, the move was written down and placed in a tube on the bird's leg and released to fly back to the lands of their enemy.

The King retired, walking slowly along the stone corridors with his Chancellor.

"How is the Duke?" the King enquired.

"I'm afraid he may die," the Chancellor replied. "He was inflicted with a vile pestilence from the bites of fleas, as you know."

"He was my last ally. Without him there will be another kind of war," said the King.

"The game will not suffice?"

"The game saves lives," said the King, "not the honour of old men. We play checkers, draughts, call it what you will. They play the same and call it Jeu Force. Win or lose, there are those who still wish for blood."

The King paused by the window and watched the young Lords practice with their hawks.

"And the prize?" the Chancellor asked.

"A border town. It has good access to the river and has value on the trade routes."

"Will they win?"

"If they do, in months we will have won it back again. Nothing changes."

"Except the Duke," the Chancellor replied.

The King paused and turned to face his old friend.

"This is the world we live in. We war with pigeons, hunt with hawks and murder with fleas. There are no battles thanks to the game, but there is war nonetheless."

The Chancellor nodded in agreement.

"When the Duke dies, have his bed beaten out, collect the fleas and bring them to me in a sealed jar."

"You have something in mind, your Majesty?"

The King thought of the pigeon's leg, the tube that was flown to the castle of his enemy to be delivered to their Generals.

"I may have," the King replied.

The flying bird brings the message: If one is not extremely careful, somebody may come up from behind and strike him. The flying bird leaves him. Misfortune.

After Completion

63. Chi Chi

On Monday I was in the King's Arms on Roupell Street when I heard. Mister Prentice had been summoned to see the board of the bank and had been turned out onto the street. There had been rumours of his low behaviour. I should know; I started them.

He was the last. One by one the alley girls had plied their wicked trade and ruined the reputations of some very fine gentlemen indeed.

Lizzie sat next to me and chuckled into her pint. She gripped the glass with both of her tiny hands and wiped the foam from her lips with her stained lace gloves.

"So, what you going to do now, Tommy?"

"Thomas," I corrected her. I pulled my tattered hat down and my rag coat tighter around my work suit. I couldn't let anyone see me here.

"I'll be manager now," I said. "They've got no-one left to ask."

"Naughty boy," Lizzie said. "You got a shilling for the girl who knows what you did?"

I gave her the coin; there was always another shilling to keep this one quiet.

"Thanks, lovey," she said. "I can get a Hansom back to Soho Square now. Don't want to wear myself out before I get to work. And you'll have a shilling for me next time you see me, an' all," she said.

I said nothing and took another draught of my beer as Lizzie let the door slam behind her.

"I can't keep giving out shillings," I thought, "the books won't balance and someone'll come sniffing."

"Maybe I should see a doctor," I thought.

On Tuesday Lizzie took more of my money and caught a Hansom to the square. I'd set her up on a date with a friend of mine. Thinking of others, in my book, costs nothing. Not even a shilling.

He's ever so grateful, my fine gentleman friend. He says he needs the practice.

[Parts of Lizzie Jackson's body were found in the Thames between 31st May and 25th June 1889. It is supposed by some, but not proven, that she was Jack the Ripper's tenth victim.]

Thus the superior man takes thought of misfortune and arms himself against it in advance. Inferior people must not be employed. The finest clothes turn to rags. Be careful all day long.

Before Completion

64. *Wei Chi*

Once, a white fox came to the banks of a great river and saw the brown of the muddy water and the backs of the crocodiles that lay in wait for an unwary traveller.

For a day and a night he watched the water and paced up and down the bank looking for a way to cross until, on the second day, a crocodile slid onto the bank and spoke to the fox.

"I can take you on my back," the crocodile said, "If you only had something to give me in exchange."

The fox asked what a crocodile could possibly want.

"On the other bank of this river is a village, and in this village lives a man, and that man uses his spear to hunt me and my brothers as we lie sleeping on the shore," the crocodile said.

"If you bring the man to the river while we pretend to sleep then we can catch him and eat him and live safely. If you do this you may cross."

The fox agreed and stood upon the crocodile's back and crossed the river. But, as he approached the far bank, he thought of the crocodile's sharp, untrustworthy teeth so jumped off too soon, and dipped his tail into the water, turning the fur quite brown.

In the village the man listened to the fox's story.

"But," the man said, "white foxes are a good omen and mean no harm to us even though they are still foxes, and brown foxes are cunning killers and would have lied to the crocodile and would never have come to tell me this story. You are neither white nor brown, so I thank you for the warning but I cannot trust you."

So the man, confident in his beliefs and secure in his understanding of omens, ignored the evidence of his own eyes and went to the river with his spear to see the waiting crocodiles for himself.

And left the fox alone with his chickens.

Before Completion. Success. But if the little fox, after nearly completing the crossing, Gets his tail in the water, There is nothing that would further.

145

The Fortune Teller

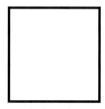

65. Suàn mìng rén

The old man looked up from his coins and yarrow stalks and smiled.

"A Prince, did you say?" he asked.

"Yes, that's right," the young man said as he sat on a cushion. "I thought I should ask you something, for my father's sake."

The old man patted the Prince's hand. "For your father? What is it?"

"He is afraid I will not come home, that the task I have set myself and my men is foolhardy and ill-advised."

"And what does he want from me?"

"He consulted you some years ago and married my mother because of it. He believes that if you tell my fortune and it is good, all will be well."

"And what do you think?" the old man asked.

"I have learned everything I can. My men are well trained, well fed and loyal. Our horses are fit and well shod. I am prepared."

"Then, here is your fortune," the old man said. He reached a frail hand into the bag at his feet, drew out a scroll of paper and placed in on the table between them.

The Prince held an edge and pulled the paper open.

"There's nothing on it," the Prince said.

"Here," the old man said, handing the Prince a brush. "You will need this."

The Judgement.

The footsteps of the Prince's own life will bring him here.
For those who possess knowledge,
The path forward,
Is as clear as the full moon.

The Image.

The curtain is drawn back to reveal the stars,
Their light falls on the curious Prince:
The image of the Fortune-Teller.

The Lines.

Neither Six nor Nine in any place means:

The fortune-teller approaches the Prince,
Bringing neither good news nor bad,
Only a way for the Prince to see himself.
No blame.

The Prince who hears only his own voice,
Has no need of six coins,
Or a bushel of yarrow stalks.
Misfortune.

The Prince may choose not to seek his fortune in signs and symbols,
But further his life with determination,
And listen to his trusted advisers,
Perseverance furthers.

Notes

28. *Ta Kuo - Preponderance of the Great* - This story, retitled "***A Handful***", first appeared as the First Prize Winner of the 2013 National Flash-Fiction Day 100 Words Competition and was published in the 2013 Anthology ***Scraps***.
ISBN 978-0-9572713-4-0

37. *Chia Jên - The Family (The Clan)* - This story, retitled "***Hope In The Snow***", first appeared as a winning entry in the ***1000Words*** 2013 National Flash-Fiction Competition.
http://1000words.org.uk/hope-in-the-snow/

40. *Hsieh - Deliverance* - This story, retitled "***The Almond Crumb Sofa***", first appeared as an official selection for the 2013 National Flash-Fiction Day Anthology, ***Scraps***.
ISBN 978-0-9572713-4-0

51. *Chên* - The Arousing (Shock, Thunder) – This story, retitled "***Bumpin' Uglies***", first appeared as an official selection on the ***FlashFlood*** blog for National Flash Fiction Day 2013.
http://flashfloodjournal.blogspot.co.uk/2013/06/bumpin-uglies-by-tim-stevenson.html

52. Kên - Keeping Still, Mountain - This story, retitled "**Alterations**", first appeared as a "Highly Commended" entry in the 2012 National Flash-Fiction Day 100 Word Story Competition and was published in the 2012 Anthology **Jawbreakers**.
ISBN: 978-1-84914-285-4

62. Hsiao Kuo - Preponderance of the Small – This story, retitled "**Birds Of Play**", first appeared as a winning entry in the **1000Words** 2013 National Flash Fiction Competition. http://1000words.org.uk/birds-of-play/

65. Suàn mìng rén - The Fortune Teller – This symbol and its meaning does not exist in the original *I Ching* text, it is my own addition to the pattern.

Made in United States
North Haven, CT
28 April 2022

18706929R00093